To Brony

Renegade Blue

By Mark Halliday

*With lots of love
and thanks*

*hope you enjoy
the read my friend*

Hovercat Books

*Luv

Mark
x*

ISBN-13: 9781543039764

ISBN-10: 1543039766

Chapter 1

Here we go.

I've spent the last forty eight hours in stasis on the far side of Collins 5. My belly is solid with zene tea mashed with flaky pastry and after six hazy weeks of relentless tracking and tracing, cross examining three hundred and fifty five databases and two hundred and eighty four infobanks I've finally got him.

I eased the 5Si across the North Pole. Unfortunately I couldn't see the fabulous two mile high glaciers, as there was a hell of a blizzard screaming across the ice sheets. Drilling winds swirled the snow upwards into ascending spirals. I shot into the thermosphere, following the trail of the Stagg freighter. Like an obelisk turned on its side she stretched deeper into space. The ship had moved far enough from the planet's departure zone to make the jump. I selected the hail column on my craft's comms panel and accelerated towards the port side.

The 5Si Gunship is a slippery vessel in combat, has a reasonably lethal load of spearfish missiles and twin microneutron cannons. A double turret between the dorsal fins keeps any rear-sneakery at bay. I even thought about buying a decommissioned one for my own purposes.

The colossal freighter slowed to allow me entry. I manually guided the 5Si to the underbelly, all spikes and ridges, where one of three circular portals slid open. Inside the ship's docking pads were three other craft, two escape modules and an Ivanian Interceptor. Freighters these size usually have sufficient armour and firepower to see off the usual privateer or opportunistic scavengers, why this handy backup?

I was greeted by a Giggesthen when I disembarked. The huge eye sunk in his belly fixed me with an even look-too even. The soles of my feet prickled. He knew who I was and why I stood on the floor of his ship.

'Pre field oscillation inspection. Just need to go through a few checks,' I declared.

He didn't reply. He held an observant stare then his eye returned the frozen gawp. I closed my nasopharynx to deter the ghastly odour which curled from his glands.

We took the conveyor platform between bridge and the cargo decks. The Giggesthen said nothing, moved little and stank terribly. All the clean air from my nostrils was sucked dry. I tried to inhale as delicately as possible.

They were transporting DS capsules to the Costello system, packed with mild sedatives; nothing to get windy about. Squadrons of capsules stood in rank upon endless rank of stacked pallets. I sifted through the log: A few minor Zonal offences for slight overloading, a caution for overzealous planetary departure.

We rode the length of the lower deck. I held my Sondisc at arms' length. The white veridical light remained constant. As we neared the stern a low box, shorter in width to the pallets sat half hidden in shade. The white light vanished, replaced by a flashing red.

'What's this?' I pointed.

A putrid waft caught me unawares. My mouth filled with saliva as I pushed my stomach back into place.

'It's a, just a couple of souvenirs.'

I stepped off the platform, relieved to exit the noxious cloud of Giggesthen body odour.

'Could you open it please?'

After further prevarication and futile perfunctory gestures he pulled the release hatch and the lid hissed open. As I unscrewed the inner safety film a dense shadow filled my chest.

Packed in loose wrapping were a collection of handmade statuettes and antique jewelry; necklaces, rings and bracelets inlaid with precious coloured stones and valuable metals.

Beside the artifacts were neatly stacked piles of scrolls, parchment and bundles of bound hide books. Filling nearly half the crate were sealed packets of hundreds of microdrives, probably the sum total of Collins' recorded culture, science and history.

I closed the lid.

'Well?'

'It all legal,' the Giggesthen slobbered.

'No, it's not *illegal*, no.'

The only sound in the deck was the low hum of the engines on breeze mode. I found myself trying to stop the hot cloud rising in my bowels. A thick smile poured across the Giggesthen's bloated belly. I peered beyond his bulk, searching for someone else I could question.

The crew was either asleep or on duty in some remote area of the vessel.

'Crew busy?' I enquired in my best casual tone. 'I'd like to interview the First Mate.' A sharp slap stung my toes. Something wasn't ticking.

He squelched towards me wriggling his elementary finger.

'In his cabin. Felt sick before takeoff.'

'May I see him? I'll make it brief, then, you can continue your delivery.'

He oozed and rumbled as his eye bounced in random directions. My feet felt like they were being bitten by a Kron plant. The platform whisked us three decks up and four corridors from the bridge.

The door of his cabin displayed a bright striplight above the threshold. 'What's his name again?' The Giggesthen mumbled a reluctant answer.

I leaned close to the communication aperture.

'Stenzen, I need to ask you a few questions. Won't take long.'

The intercom remained static, a silent ring of metallic bumps.

'Stenzen this is Sheriff Luten, may I come in? If you –'

'Maybe he's sleeping?'

The great eye puckered, the belly swelled between me and the door.

'Open it.'

The eye retreated deep into a cleavage of damp blubber. Grumbling in his own tongue he passed a tendril across the door. In place of the first mate stood pearlescent refrigerant crates. All were missing the orbital exit stamp. The Giggesthen sat still, pooling in his hill of flesh. I lifted a hand towards the nearest crate. His eye was wrinkled tight.

'Look I can call a dozen sheriffs and a provost here in an eye blink.'

He squelched; a rubbery slurp.

'How do you want to play it?'

The eye squinted. The room filled with sulphurous fury. The soles of my feet were splitting in two.

He pressed the security clearance. I scanned the contents.

'Sken embryos?'

His gelatinous bulk stopped frigid.

I closed the lid.

'What's the problem?' a new voice demanded.

I turned to face the first mate, a Terran, *human*, possibly from Lennon 9 (a flourishing colony of exiles and retired mercenaries) judging by the skin tone and hair texture.

'There's no exit stamp.' I allowed my words to sink in, playing the queens hand, then I added, 'you know what these things grow up to be, right?'

The Giggesthen's eyelid was half closed in contempt. The Terran made a move to close the lid. I positioned myself between the fridge and his hand. He stepped back, locking his arms together.

'And here you are sheriff, all badge and breeze boots with a Sondisc by your guts.'

From my periphery I could discern the Giggesthen shuddering with mirth. The hot cloud burst into white heat in my thorax. I had to squeeze every atom of willpower to stop myself stabbing that glittering orb with his ragged tendrils which were waving tantalisingly before my face.

Now, the human was playing the professional khak stirrer, keeping his masked insults within permissible boundaries while those derisive tendrils wormed closer. I could cuff them for contempt…

however in this star system he could exercise his right to Multiverse Expression.

The three of us stood there in the cabin, each of us locked in our own patch of grudging principles. I willed myself calm. They had me, the embryos weren't strictly contraband, but that fridge had no stamp.

I didn't recognise my voice when it spoke; it trembled and had gone up a couple of notches.

'I'll have to impound those embryos. There is no export certificate and besides they aren't contained in secure transit.'

I removed my Sondisc and began to signal the nearest Stellaport.

'What are you doing?' the man threatened, a dangerously calm voice. He had been glowering in my ear. I could feel the electric fizz radiate from his beige face.

'A BZi unit will arrive shortly to collect these embryos and examine the artifacts below deck.'

The human being exploded.

'This is you shits all over! What have you got against us making a cut, eh? Do-gooding drones like you, spoiling everyone's right to a bit of starshine, just because you've neither the guts nor the brains to do what we do.'

'Sir, if you calm down, please, this does no one any good. No need for vulgar language.' My legs were fairly shaking. I gripped the Sondisc tight until my cerulean fingers turned a pale periwinkle.

As I pressed my forefinger to activate the transponder frequency he lunged for the gold disc. Although my stomach was churning the water to acid I reflexively grabbed his wrist. Pulling his momentum towards me I twisted hard, thrust my right leg bag and swiveled my hips, turning him sideways and flying straight into the embryo crates. The containers clattered to the floor, spilling the contents over the gleaming grey marble effect floor.

The Giggesthen swiped a claw for my shoulder. I couldn't deflect the blow in time. Fortunately these shoulder pads are reinforced. With his claw embedded in my uniform, I raised my disc. A ripple of psionic energy hit the eye, sending him reeling into a thick puddle in the furthest corner.

The human landed a couple of heavy shots in my side. Before his third punch landed I snatched his wrist again, intending to deaden the arm into an elbow lock. I adjusted my stance and froze in violent disorientation. My foot slipped on amniotic fluid and we both splashed to the floor, writhing and struggling.

We were quickly soaked in the soupy liquid, rolling and wrestling to gain any significant advantage. The human was stronger than I. Most of them usually are, and I was weakening due to months of inertia and lukewarm junk food.

 He was trying to bite me but I had a firm hold of his throat. He gnashed and nudged his jaw to chomp my hand. The strength was draining from my forearm and his left hand was reaching between my legs; which was held in check by my sharp elbow and upper arm.

Then his arm seemed to snake free of my block and he struck a hard hook into the side of my head. There wasn't enough space to pack any muscle behind the fist but he made a clubbing effort, enough to make the space in my skull whine and my lithe body to vibrate.

He was on his feet kicking me in the sides. I held my hands before my face while slithering in the amniotic fluid to hunch tighter. The hormones which flushed through me when the fight began were running dry. I felt supremely exhausted and feared for my life. My

Sondisc was lying beside a crate, alive with blinking lights and crackling voices.

The human made a half step backwards. The next kick would be the killer.

He swung his foot fast toward my head as if kicking a leisure ball. My eyes could only watch in solid anticipation of the boot shooting in line with my exposed skull.

When the tip of his toe began its sweeping rise my Sondisc faded quietly into the background, the lights dimmed and the importuning voice sounded far off or sounded as if it were speaking underwater. The walls of the cabin blurred and the growing pains in my body gently receded. The human was the room, the freighter and the surrounding vacuum. Even the cold discomfort of the gelling amniotic fluid clung like a second skin.

The toe grew in immensity and was achingly suspended between my contracting vision and the brittle shell of my skull. My hand reached out with effortless concern, the fingers curling around the man's sole, assisting the flight of the boot and with a slight push diverted the foot away and above my head, lifting the leg in an easy rise high into the air.

The sounds from the disc returned loud and clear, the walls shifted back into view and I shivered inside the layer of fluid between my uniform and skin.

He toppled backwards, hitting the base of his head on the edge of a refrigerated crate with a muffled thud. He slid fluently into the frothing puddles of bubbling embryos.

When I staggered to my feet I vaguely heard the announcement of the BZi unit making its final approach. At the precise moment the backup crew boarded the freighter I crouched into the open fridge and heaved my guts wholly into the vacant chamber.

It took three Sanito sessions and a plasma detox to cleanse the Sken filth from my flaxen hair and spongy flesh. I adjusted the water to 90 degrees: Bliss. The first shoots briefly scalded, but after my hypothalamus sorted the temperature I scraped and scrubbed until I was raw. My muscles surrendered to the heat so I could happily 'ohh' and 'ahh' my way through the scathing ablution. Following the coating of muck down the drainage slot were weeks of grime and grease, I imagined the human and Giggesthen being sucked into the gurgling slit and immediately felt much better.

After I sent my report to the Lord Provost, I settled into my shallow vibrapool while the llenmn plants from my home world sang me into a somatic repose.

I made a vaco beef casserole with fried ilchips. As the ilchips browned I surveyed the flashing city far below. I live high above, among the dazzling signs and emblems, logos and crests. Skiffs and shuttles zipped between destinations before the flowering adverts above our heads, Millions of glaring lights, mostly lily white in colour, dotted the vast canyon of apartments, office blocks and public service provisions. In under one year I can sell my nest and move on, 125 000 credits bigger and safely far from the maddening crowd.

Millions of beings forever occupied: Conning, hustling, conniving, conspiring, stealing, falsifying, punching, stabbing and shooting. Every day hundreds of enforcement droids would file out onto our teeming streets and return with smashed visors, an arm or three missing, crushed, crumpled and covered in waste that would leave forensics scratching their heads. Some never returned at all: Probably sold as parts to an asset stripper.

I scoffed the meal heartily, had another wash and settled into my spacious bed. I caught the highlight of the plasmoball game. I'd never been a fan of sports but a fellow sheriff wheedled me into betting on the outcome of an important match. We won and I'd stuck with the team for the last two years. We were doing reasonably well, keeping within touching distance with the league leaders in the local Shield. They had recently been bought by unknown investor and were able to buy the best pilots, ships and latest upgrades. The media outlets adored them because the captain, a smug Frolornoan, all shiny eyed and blemish free, had goaded our squadron leader into a petty spat over recent decisions which they obsequiously referred to in their interviews with him while taunting our own leader on the points gap. He thought he was Kon's gift to the game and whenever he insulted a reporter they'd masochistically congratulate him on his "genius." Their electromagnetic cannons used for shooting the plasma ball into the goal zone were also suspiciously over powered and their skate ships never seemed to malfunction. We were up against a struggling side that lost five games in a row. The statistics and success ratios suggested a conclusive victory by ten or twenty goals. We started off racing down the flanks of the arena pining them back into a defensive line. We bombarded the goal, shot after innumerable shot, at times drawing back to the halfway line to enforce a counter attack but they never moved, preferring to pile their skate ships in a heap so tight a single neuron would have returned in shame. The second half was much the same except in the final seconds of play we won an infringement. The goal was open and clear. Our captain, who'd scored in every infringement this season swerved around in a wide arc lining up his sights. The ball was hovering between him and three crucial points. He sped towards the spot, released a full volley of cannon, hitting the ball at an impossible angle for the top corner.

The game ended 0-0.

Dreamless sleep blanketed me before I could properly wallow in yesterday's glorious coup and a regretful opportunity to catch the Shield leaders.

My chest swelled as I inspected my spindly body snug inside the blue and yellow chevrons of the Syndicate uniform. I ate a spare breakfast, my stomach was barreling and my throat was rigid with eager anticipation. The Lord Provost requested a personal sitting.

Today. 10:00.

I could hardly keep my silver spearhead skiff within the recommended velocity. Weaving between two conical insurance offices, The Justice of the Peace Courts slipped into view three hundred metres below me, surrounded by rivers of life forms streaming to their appetent designations. I powered through twin holographic adverts for instant credit and free membership of a gambling consortium.

On my descent trajectory the surface gates opened in the courtyard. I dipped inside the underground docking bay, logging the skiff close to the elevators.

My stomach bubbled grumpily: A rip, a high squeal, the yawning drop in the bowels. No, not now not today. Silence. Stillness: A single pop, a dull ricochet. The nearest toilets were along the next corridor. I crunched my abdominals, keep it in…hold it in. Maintain a gastronomical ceasefire.

What followed was a twenty one gun salute.

My weary resignation turned to annoyance. I just put clean underwear on…

Hurrying down the corridors I politely removed myself from the skiff attendants, calling behind my shoulder I'd be back to square the log in. Faa…why is this place so packed. You never pass more than a maintenance droid these days. Why has the entire Syndicate turned out to cheer on my marathon bum shuffle?

Get out of the way I whined to myself. The pain in my guts outweighed any dignity left so I opened my legs and chanced a loping run.

Good job I left early. I had to dump my underwear. At least my belly was content, settled now in its empty pot. I sat on the toilet seat nearly in tears. I toyed with the notion of returning home and jacking in this patchy affair.

Six of years of fruitless observation reports, lane co-ordination and accident inquiries dulled my initial love of the job. For the past three months during my pursuit of the Giggesthen freighter I mused over the possibility of leaving the Judiciary and starting my own private consultancy. Thankfully, impounding that Stagg ship has probably earned me a stiff term with Peacekeeping or Narcotic Ops.

After a swift scrub and wipe I climbed the polished steps to the Procurator's office. The last time I was here was to collect my silver badge. Sitting deep in my guts a hot ball pulsed. A felony escort shuttled overhead, fresh from the morning hearings. A troupe of youthful sheriffs clattered downstairs, intoxicated with two weeks leave and the bottle of Blandaflu they passed around. A handful of sheriffs joined me in the long climb. The sleek columns shone bright in the weak sunlight pressing us through the lintel bearing the shield of office – a Daltrey mantis and humanoid bearing an eight pointed star within a circle/. We paraded through the entrance, heading for the door marked 'Authorised Personnel Only.'

I announced my arrival to the veneered screen and the door opened silently.

Time: 9:59:34.

Seated behind a desk the size of a cruiser's hull panel was The Procurator Fiscal, Lord Advocate and an unfamiliar face seated at an impossibly obtuse angle. This is it: Promotion? Brilliant: A Commission…Warm foam burst forth in my firm belly.

I stood before my superior at ease. From my peripheral vision the nebulous shapes flanking him remained immobile and vaguely sentient. My boss pinioned his wiry arms, resting his pincers on the matt surface of the desk. Before he spoke his mandibles clicked.

'Luten, do you realise the cataclysmic blinder you have wrought upon us?'

I stood still; at ease. I could sense my lack of a surname was already distending his already puffed thorax.

'Not only did you fail to recover the smuggled artifacts, you slaughtered hundreds of valuable life forms. Mr. Macbeth-' he snapped a jagged claw towards the unknown presence '-is considering suing for loss of merchandise and willful damage to his property, namely one Mk III interstellar freighter. It is by the providence of our Lord Advocate you aren't sitting in an isolation booth two hundred metres below this office and we aren't fishing for next years' budget in the trash drives.'

He reclined in his high backed chair, lowering his obsidian eyes on the desktop which flicked on a triptych of three scowling faces.

'I have no idea how you graduated. Your only quasi skill frankly astonishes me. I have no doubt these abilities overshadowed your other modules in attaining that badge. I don't know how you managed to pass through the initial self authorship filters and productivity checks but that's another bundle of wires to untangle. Your performance indicators are well below average, you show minimal impact on arrest statistics and have yet to engage in any committee initiative. However, your professional review is due shortly, so, we shall reflect on your tenure with us and future outcome until then. In the meantime, you shall trace and return three fugitives. Jumped from their incarceration region yesterday, hijacked a frigate and have vanished completely. Disappeared without trace. You will be assigned a new partner to assist you. That is all.'

The desktop changed back to matt black. I saluted and about faced. When I reached the door the Procurator called 'The only reason you have been assigned this mission is because the leader of these renegades is one of your own.'

So that was that.

Chapter 2

As the door clicked shut I stood in the corridor, staring with frozen eyes upon the teeming streets, holding the window rail to prevent my legs folding and slamming me in an untidy heap on the polished floor. The field of usual questions lay fallow.

I negotiated my way through the bustling corridors, heading for the itech suite. My *quasi* skill?

He was obviously referring to the Karel case. In my final year at the Academy I was attached to a murder investigation. High officials in the Zenden prefecture were found either plain dead without an atom of evidence, motivation or trace of weapon. Some were discovered with their rectums bored clean with their spinal cords removed. Others were eyeless, the brains removed without a sign of implement or tool used in the process.

I was assigned to a cohort of marshalls sent to investigate the most recent death. A moderator found in his T Cruiser with not a drop of blood left in his shriveled body. There were no puncture marks, nor any indication of coronary surgery.

As soon as I stepped near the heaped corpse faint jagged impressions clouded my thoughts: A fourth dimensional being, pulsing sharply without any recognisable form or discernable language. I searched hyperspace for weeks, sitting for up to nine hours a day, mind displaced in an abstract plane far removed from vaco beef casserole and racy skiffs.

Finally, between two star clusters within the Andromeda galaxy, I picked up an anomalous splurge of dark matter. Edging toward the energy, I felt the vibration sense my approach. We both considered each other, the mass of waves, pulses and particles. All I could do was to collate as much intel as I could remember while we faced off. I needed at least a whole day to complete the re-entry process in my body. The following month while I recovered my senses the murders stopped and I graduated with a 3.1in my attainment criteria, barely able to keep my eyes open through the morning ceremony.

My eyes caught a snaking movement approaching the hustling stream of sheriffs, engineers, administration cyborgs and auxiliary staff: A young female Kitt. One of the least appealing life forms in this sector. She stopped immediately, a direct halt of her slinking, smirking face.

'Hello, nice to be working with you.'

She offered me her hand which I brushed with my palm. I hurried away blowing the distance between me and the Procurator as my lean legs could walk.

She insisted on brushing against my arms, sometimes placing a foot before me sometimes dropping behind with no reasonable cause. Her eyes were typical Kitten: Auriferous lime alternating between cute and primal cunning. A portion of her right ear was missing her delicate chin lightly furred. She walked upright, wearing a modified probationer tunic. Her hands were shaped with fingers and palms rather than pads and claws from the majority of felines from Kitt 1. They hung beside her hocks, loose and curled. I'd met a few in the Academy: I hoped I'd never meet another in a long time.

The isuite was packed. My disc needed charging so I had to manually upload the mission brief in a booth between a rancid Klegh and an overweight humanoid whose corpulent waist kept pushing me towards the miasma of the Klegh's respiratory organs. They are brilliant deep space navigators and undertake a lot of dangerous solo work undercover no doubt blending in superbly with other swamp inhabitants and gaseous beings. There was a tinge of aro spice blended with pheromones discharging from his boggle eyed face skimming the memo updates. I held my tiny nostril shut to thwart the stench from infesting my lungs and corrupting the soul. There were a dozen memos waiting in my inbox. I hadn't the time to waste trawling through them so we descended to the departure platform.

While we waited on our allocated ship we stopped in the lounge. She ordered a Lactodrene, I, a mineral juice.

I outlined the brief, suggesting we interview eye witnesses and search the tracking router for the frigate's wake. She sunk half the cup, licking her lips: That smug smile never leaving that feline face. My disc hummed. Our ship was prepared.

'Right. Let's go.'

She remained seated, both legs folded under her hips.

'Haven't we forgotten something?'

I retraced the mission guidelines, the curt directive; the boss' orders. Investigate and apprehend three escaped terrorists. Proceed by flying to Lennon 3, interrogate any witnesses, guards or other prisoners.

I'd spent three years on Lennon 3, in Denver. I could speak three or four of their languages competently. I knew the elementary rituals and customs of the purgatory sector. This seemed the logical place to start and I assumed my time on the planet combined with one of the fugitives being my own species would fit the profile of my choice as prime officer for this mission.

'No, what?' I asked.

Her smile tightened raising those prominent cheekbones revealing a brilliant fang.

'What's your name?'

Typical Kitt nonsense. I wasn't in an appropriate mood for their esoteric mind games. She would have gleaned my name from her own supervisory commander. Though within the dusty recesses in my skull I guessed this might be my last days in a sheriff uniform if this mission fell below expectations judging by the boss' snappy attitude. Best play along.

'Luten.'

'I'm Lyrae Tcheetz,'

The fuzzy face pushed her hand across the table. Her palms were rough, the fingers covered in downy fur. She squashed my fingers in a firm shake. I spotted the openings where her claws were retracted. As our contact was released five tiny clear tips peeped out from the holes. She's enjoying this the-

'Pleased to meet you. Now, the ship?'

'Oh, sure.'

When the aftershock of the Procurator's proclamation faded my eyes settled on her badge.

A trainee.

A harsh scrape against my buttocks reminded me of more pertinent concerns.

'See here, I've some classified business I need to address urgently. Wait here, I'll be back shortly.' I scurried out, waddled for two blocks until I found a cheap garment store. With clean underwear tucked under my arm I nipped back into the Justice building, shot into the staff changing rooms and emerged six minutes later feeling like new skin.

The Kitten hadn't moved a whisker.

We descended into hangar 8, the level where long range and intergalactic ships were docked. These underground hangars are cities themselves with maintenance avenues and test districts

.Extending into the distance were streets of battle cruisers, destroyers, frigates and smaller long range patrol craft. We headed for gate 9E where an entire chasm was decorated with blue and yellow chevrons, stripes and checks. Corvette 5Ti was fully charged and armed and eagerly awaiting our departure. The Kitt's eyes followed me as I lead the way.

'Getting a bit cold eh? Even the sun feels like it's deserting us.'

She was referring to the shaft of air charging in through the gates, kept open during the first quarter of the day.

'All to do with the tilt of the planet.'

'No I mean the temperature.'

'Well, the heat *is* rising above us.'

She giggled behind a clenched fist.

Maybe I should have resigned after all.

The corvette's Regulyn II chip completed the pre-flight checks and self assessment log. The mission statement was uploaded and when four green lights showing peak performance appeared in a row on the lower fascia (engine/weapons/communication and navigation systems) we confirmed the destination and settled ourselves for the two day journey. Rows of guidance beacons drove through the dimly lit hangar. The engine filled with power and we were off.

The only chink of light touching my gloom was the pleasure in piloting a corvette. A medium sized attack ship, it can operate as a battle craft, is used for long range convoys and pursuit, has intergalactic capability and the cargo hold is large enough to transport twenty suspects. The two pilots can sleep, wash and eat in the small ante cabin and it has armour and shields to rival a frigate and can outgun most pirates and minor cruisers. Oh, and it flies like a raging comet.

Our ship slipped through both hangar portals, accelerating from the Syndicate Station into the atmosphere past a hive of construction droids repairing the new flight simulation installation, hundreds of lights swarming furiously above the crenellated skyline below.

The roof of the Court building proudly bore the title ASS: Associated Species Syndicate.

We climbed higher, propelling high above the planet, leaving the shrinking urban patch as a stain on the continent. When we breached space we passed a gang of single seat V tail canoes. I ran a check and they were cleared. They were only youths having a race around Donovan's stratospheric boundaries.

The corvette eagerly left the Donovan system, gathering speed before shifting bearings. When navigation aligned coordinates the communication sensors surveyed local and remote stellar pathways. Satisfied the flight stream was clear our engine initiated the Einstriv, the ion accelerator whooshed into life and we were sucked into Paraspace.

A spectral whirlpool engulfed the cabin screens and monitors: This was a routine transit but I always offered a thought of hope we wouldn't be vacuumed into an antimatter spiral and find ourselves as two amoebas, sitting in the pilot seats wondering where our next meal was coming from.

The Kitten reclined in her seat. Her eyes were closed while she purred, extending her claws from the fingers of both hands. The musky whiff clogged my throat. I wanted to spit the smell from my mouth. I hadn't washed my hands since we left the lounge. First toilet break and I'd give them a thorough scrub.

We re-entered visible space close to Lennon 3. This star system's contribution to the Association was excellent music and superb food.

The Sun cast a sphere of blinding energy across the system: The radiant arms touching every planet within reach.

My memories of Lennon 3 resurfaced rapidly. Cuts, bites, stings, scratches, swellings, headaches, diseases, viruses, infections, rashes, strains and pains and sores, lumps, bumps and mumps, coughs, sneezes, wheezes and fevers, altitude sickness, constipation and diarrhea: Often concurrently. Whatever passed by I picked it up. Oh, and hemorrhoids like asteroids.

I spent a year in Colorado, outside Denver. During my father's penultimate season with the Council's diplomatic division I rarely attended my classes. I was the only non-terrestrial and didn't they let me know. From the thousand glaring eyes burning my nerves to ash as I padded across the courtyards, to the tumbling corridors with their daily wrestling bouts, I tried to shrink inside the glazed walls. My head peeped above everyone else's of course and would frequently be a target for a hugely resourceful array of missiles. When a squirt of pepper sauce narrowly missed my right eye I abandoned the daily trial. The final straw was when I was hauled off to the biopsycho facilitator after my third warning for misbehaviour.

I sat curling my toes and clasping my fingers into a whitening basket as I heard him explain my incorrigible deviance to my parents.

'Yes, well Luten is severely dysfunctional. His patterning shows signs of inefficacious cognition syndrome.'

I heard my father's robes rustle. He cleared his throat asking 'What is wrong with him Mr. Neville?'

'He is a social fugitive sir.'

'But, what is the problem, please?'

23

'He daydreams sir.'

 Although I soaked up a dozen languages and enjoyed cultural studies I would spend lazy afternoons with a crowd of similarly bored and itchy drop outs. My new gang didn't spit in my violet eyes or lie in wait with eager feet and fists. We surfed across the mountains, mooched around the outer wilderness of the Denver Stella where we punished our waking hours with huge quantities of mescadrine.

Whistle and Kent knew of an old mine shaft where a stash of genuine MJ was hidden.

'The only deal man, is it's like down the old mine shaft.'

'So?'

'The door, the hole…the what is it the shaft man, it's too narrow,'

They all considered my two metre tall skinny frame and the deal was done.

We walked for an hour across semi desert taking turns to carry a heavy drum of water which the boys guzzled heartily. When our boots weren't sinking in the soft grains our toes were jabbed by the nail hard cactus. Whistle pointed to the entrance, fenced off by metal poles and spars. We threw the rickety barrier aside and I peered down the gullet of the mine.

'It's all total good, man, just a coupla feet down.'

 My feet were prickly and it wasn't from the cactus spines.

I placed one foot gingerly on the first rung which held firm. Lowering myself down into the darkness I couldn't feel the next rug.

 'It's awright man, juss solid earth now.'

I let go the ladder and was jolted by the hard landing, I couldn't see a thing before me.

'It's like there man, total feel around.'

I fumbled and caressed the gritty surface, skirting the walls of the shaft.

'I can't find it I called,' looking up.

There, standing around the square of light were my four friends all with their trousers around their ankles.

'Drink this ya blue asshole.'

The ropes of urine hit me square in the face.

I yelled and pleaded as the piss pitter pattered on my head, drenching my shoulders and hair. The dry ground turned to shallow mud while I waited, covering my face as I was showered with squirts. When the boys left I waited until the urine dried where I returned late at night to deeply concerned parents and the Embassy whose walls I never left until we returned to Elyssia the following spring.

The only time I would dare venture out was the final six or seven weekends and only then with my hovercraft. I would fly deep into the San Luis valley where I sheltered among a creaking collection of cabins and shacks, contemporary domes and a quiet bar nestled among the cactus and pinon trees. The people were mellow, subsisting on local produce; beans, squash and scrawny chickens. Their electricity was supplied by a waterwheel dynamo from the nearby creek. On dry days it could have been the year 6018 or 1860. I'd sit sampling the local brew, suffering terrifying hangovers for days afterward. I talked with the locals absorbing their customs and habits. One morning the barkeeper brought a box filled with musty paperbacks sealed in a preserved capsule, I read the entire stock of detective fiction and westerns with my beer and burgers. From then on it was hotdogs with Shakespeare, pizza with Poe and curry with Conan Doyle devoured to the songs of Leadbelly and Robert Johnson.

One evening in the splintered saloon I ordered a double with my beer. The cluster of bruises on my face needed strong medicine. I brooded on fantastic revenge tragedies, pondered assassination scenarios and murder scenes.

'Been in the wars again son?'

His beefy belly must have been twice my body weight. He spoke as if he held time at his disposal and as if the listener all the patience of the day. We bought each other a chain of shots and soon the bar was filled with our empty bottles. When, after the requisite gallons were drunk, sunk and pissed he asked about my deep purple wounds. I slurred out my woes with only an hour remaining. Over the clanging last bell I heard him drawl:

'Let it pass, son. Let it pass.'

He always wore the same replica shirt which never got dirty. I'd find him out felling trees or skinning the remains of his prey. He was a retired sheriff and one of the few humans I spoke more than ten words to. He held us fixated with his tales of pirate busting and tracking the galaxy's most dangerous for months on end. All delivered as if he were reciting the contents of his supper. He took me hikes up mountains and polished my aim. It was a dear if unusual friendship with more than a few morning hangovers.

I bought him a heavy hunting knife one day, settled in with two beers waiting until closing time. I tried to pace myself, sipping the beer in lazy intervals which increased to eventual gulps. Jonah Stark, another of our beer buddies scurried across the dusty path as the hovercraft landed to pilot me home. He rested his hands on my swaying shoulders grabbing the near empty bottle swigging the contents hard before announcing:

'It's Hank. I'm sorry Luten, he passed away this morning. His heart failed him.'

Jonah offered me Hank's badge.

'He would have wanted you to have it son. Take it.'

I accepted the silver square, which never left my pocket until we returned to Elyssia.

The corvette joined the merging lanes as Lennon 3's surface ballooned into view, sitting within the gorgeous blue seas we saw Africa, the huge heart shaped land mass flanked by the lungs of South America and India.

Lennon 3 has four continental zones. Zone 1 is commerce and administration, mostly Europe, North America and western parts of Russia. Zone 2 covers resource and fabrication, mostly what remains of Asia and Africa. Number 3, our destination, is the penitentiary zone. 4 is the megastate of Antarctica, the port of the world where our ship was stuck in a queue behind cargo vessels and commuters. I released and audible sigh.

'We can use the emergency route.'

I folded my arms. 'We are not in an emergency. Besides, regulations state…you should know this.'

'Only offering an opinion.'

We watched the exiting craft whizz from the southern poles in the thousands disappearing into splashes of blinding light as they entered Paraspace.

'Won't be long, we'll be there soon.'

An hour later we passed the damned hold up: Routine maintenance to a fusion arc. I had a mind to arrest the tardy droids for obstruction. The Kitten sat dozing, purring smugly while the corvette inched forward, creeping behind a grinning Zaepan advertising relaxing breaks on Presley 2 from the rear of an ore freighter.

By the time we cleared the sheriff portal I was ready to throttle the Kitten. Making jokes with a pink level Senator. Good, Kon…'

The duty officer walked with us into the staff parlour.

'You investigating the frigate heist?'

'Yes,' the Kitten replied, stealing my breath.

'Fine, fine I'll arrange an escort.' He was a stout humanoid, tanned: Looked like he hadn't used his disc in years. He too laughed with the Kitten. The Association employs anyone these days I mused.

We waited on orange cushioned chairs. A couple of off duty operatives stood holding the bar, halfway drunk.

Beside the doorway a civilian sat swirling the foamy dregs of his lager. Lennon 3 also brews the best beer this side of Andromeda. His grey beard was trimmed; he was balding and sat behind a solid paunch which stretched his shirt into a smooth, round ball. When he spotted us he waved. Eventually he drained his glass and limped towards our table.

'G' Day. Buy an old digger an amber?'

The Kitten cocked her head, both ears twitched independently.

'Sure get yourself a chug Put it on my tab,' I grinned.

'Cheers sport.'

He returned with a bubbling glass of lager and a cracked smile covering the lower half of his face.

'Bottoms up.'

The Kitten shifted her position, creeping closer to me while our guest gulped generous mouthfuls of his brew.

'On a sweat are yer? By the smell of yer, I'd say yer on the trail o' the three bludgers from the Mexico bust out.'

The Kitten sat casting silent disapproval. She twisted her head to the window watching a brace of patrol craft shuttling into the berthing lanes.

I leaned my elbows on the table. I liked most Australians I'd encountered here in my youth. He'd seen a fair few scraps if the melted nose was anything to judge.

'Know anything cobber?'

The frayed human swallowed his beer, wiping the froth from his moustache with a forefinger.

'Yeah, a bit. Don't know much about your blue brother but the two porkers are bad eggs. He's in league with a crew o' gangsters from Ryder 4 and she's inter cannibalism an' all sorts.'

'Are you retired?' fuzzy face cut in.

'Yup.' He finished the glass quickly.

'Why hang around here?'

'I had a good innings young mog. Trouble is when yer take off the cozzie…well, what else yer got?'

He wrapped his arm around the whole of my upper back, resting his temple on mine.

'Never leave the circle mate; there's nothin' out there but hunger an' cold nights.'

A red haired sheriff stood framing the door. He looked freshly unwrapped from Training Academy. He marched over when he saw us.

'Luten?'

'Yes?'

'I'm Spartacus. I'll take you to the Penitentiary Zone. Hogie, come on. Haven't you had enough today?'

The old man rose, suckled the dregs from the glass and limped to the exit. He turned, fixing his good eye on me.

'Good luck sport, hope yer catch 'em.' He adjusted his greasy jacket. The outback's changed, watch yer back mate,' he muttered leaving with a scowl for the Kitt and a wink for me. The young sheriff watched him depart before sitting beside us.

'I do apologise. He's harmless really. Excellent operative in his day mind.'

Spartacus booked a four seater scout craft, used mostly for planetary reconnaissance and surface patrols. When we were airborne The Kitten announced she was hungry. Spartacus and I decided we were too so after a few suggestions I concluded we try the New Savoy.

Africa scrolled beneath us. Her face alternating dry savannah and scrub to jungle to desert. France was a fifteen minute skim of green expanse with the occasional lake blemishing the countless manufacturing plants where a shift shuffled back to the same stone, wood and earth dwellings their ancestors lived albeit with better tasting coffee. The twinkle and flurry of Paris billowed around us then a blur across the English Channel where we slowed to an easy pace. London was splattered across the south east of the country, fringing the coast and dissolving into the grey cloud heavy horizon. We nipped into one of the numerous vehicle entry apertures and soon joined the flow of skiffs, leisure craft, transporters and commercial ships coasting underground in a wide tunnel gushing into the heart of the great megalopolis.

 The three of us surfaced on the Embankment. The Thames was still as I remembered: A coat of chocolate foulness oozing towards the estuary, slug like. The same old spires, columns and towers poked through the haze, a petrified forest of adrenaline speculation and gambler's prey: Where the destinies of distant worlds spun on silver discs.

This was the Kitten's first time on Lennon 3. Even she with her four years of star hopping was unused to the crammed route ways and over spilling hi-walks. She gingerly followed us, sidestepping and pausing before the onrushing stampede of legs, arms, tendrils, horns, claws, proboscis and hooves, feet, paws and tracks.

She paused before a clothing exchange as a gaggle of humans dragged their pet Agledigs on magnaleads. Some bipedal servants followed the owners into the shop. People swaggered, swayed, preened and posed in fresh outfits and hairstyles, colliding with each other and narrowly avoiding injury when they pushed each other off the path. Perfume, cologne and fast food flooded the street under the perpetual boom and blare of holoads overhead. The Kitt rejoined us, bewildered as we headed for the Savoy. Fluorescent lights flowed alongside our feet, holoads boomed above our heads and our skin tingled with the seductive lure of the omnipresent moaning pleasure domes.

We were escorted to floor fifteen, the oceanic suite. Sea shells from every shore patterned the rippling walls, the lovingly carpeted floor was a deep sandy hue and they even had real human waiters. The Kitten seemed to perk up instantly.

Spartacus leaned close to my auricle.

'Can we, you afford this?'

I released a chesty laugh, slapping his back before marshalling him to the only lonely table in the room. A compelling impulse made me look to the door. When I leveled my sight, a shadowy figure, previously standing in the frame, leapt suddenly out of view.

 While we waited for our food I rifled through the background of the three fugitives.

Sharon Agate, 23. Ostensibly an accounts manager of an education enterprise by day, purveyor of children's saliva to the inhabitants of Osbourne 6 by night. Caught by one her staff forcing a six year old to spit in a hydrotube late one winter evening in New Manchester.

Thomas Perk, 31. Cautioned for joyriding skiffs when in infancy. Jailed at 15 for GTC. Was currently serving a two year sentence for I.D. fraud...

 As I flipped the index, searching for my compatriot the projector on my disc flickered. When I selected his name, I was faced with a blank screen. I checked the power on my disc. 98%. Odd...

The steaming plates arrived: Raw salmon and fresh lobster platter for the Kitt, a well done steak for me and a measly plate of oysters for Spartacus. I trimmed the rubbery fat, opening a slice to ensure it was properly cooked before I filled my mouth with the still sizzling meat.

'I thought you Elyssians were veggie?'

I waited until small chunks of steak slipped into my belly before I replied.

'Mm. Not me. Look, these humans, they're not exactly galactic warlords. Petty crime, semi-smuggling…seems a bit off the menu for the likes of them. The Elyssian, well, I tried to upload his profile…I'll get it later.'

'I checked him out before we left. Appears out of nowhere. No record of concern, no probationary convictions, nothing. Materialised out of the vacuum. No other known accomplices or persons associated. We catch him running a load of DS petals from Hendrix 5 three weeks ago.'

'Good, good work,' I nodded, bouncing my knife on the half eaten flesh. My rectum was stiffening. Something wasn't sitting right with this one.

'Your people are ecologically cognizant. They are a nurturing species who value beauty and each other highly. Would any Elyssian know of him or his family?'

My sphincter was fibrillating avidly. A waiter asked us if we were satisfied. I nodded enthusiastically.

'Would any of your elders know about him?'

My stomach twisted sharply. A biting pain seized my abdomen. I shunted the seat back.

'You'll have to excuse me.'

I trotted to the exquisite bathroom to further masticate upon the mystery. Slamming the cubicle door I removed my trousers and jettisoned a cargo of vile toxic waste into the calm blue water. Bloody neuropeptide nonsense.

By the time my belly eventually settled and I disposed of the wipes we had crossed the Atlantic and we were gliding over the Florida Everglades. The auto-climatiser adjusted the cabin temperature as the marked change from London's cool air to humid swampland provoked us to loosen the top clips on our uniforms.

The Mexican coast rolled forwards where we saw their spectacular cliffs. The azure sea circling the coast, eroding the titanic rocks to luxuriant sand was strangely calm as if it were a captured holoimage. Tracing the coastline Spartacus guided us over the Yucatan peninsula, one of the largest penal colonies in the Zone. He brought the craft to a perfect two point landing where the three of us headed for the company administration block. After a brief wait we were ushered to the site where the Elyssian and two humans were allocated their purgatorial tasks.

We walked towards the edge of a large Cenote, a sinkhole where the indigenous people of this land once regarded as a sacred portal to the afterlife. Some were used for ritual sacrifice, often valuable items were thrown in the waters as an offering. I peered over the rim of the crater to witness a thousand or more beings of varied race, species and nationality. Most wore a collection of dusty grey overalls. Of the beings that had facial or scalp hair they were all the same cloudy pallor dusting the overalls. Their skin showed every wrinkle and their eyes were starkly liquid in both movement and gaze.

They shuffled from the depths of the pit, hugging the walls in a spiraling whirlpool of slumped shoulders and sagging faces, a vortex of bare feet and worn bones.

'You here about the esscaped sscumm?'

We all turned to the rasping voice.

A seven foot Sauroped had his clawed toes dug deep into the scorching sand. The sun was reaching its zenith. His chest swelled and the plates on his back undulated as he soaked up the glorious heat. His skin gleamed scarlet with gold flecks and he held a pacifier baton in his right hand. His other clawed the left thigh scuffing some flies from his kneecaps.

The Kitten was slightly hunched beside me. The fur on her back stiffened.

'Yes,' she growled.

The Sauroped locked eyes with her as her claws recoiled. Their respective planets were currently in fragile talks as a tentative ceasefire has held. Millions lay dead in recent wars as their civilizations were reduced to a wrecked memory but were in danger of oblivion if these two went for it. I stepped assuredly between the two.

'What happened?'

His face slowly revolved. His eyes followed moments later. He surveyed me, clutching my presence with only slightly less contempt for the Kitten.

'The Elyssian fakess sicknesss. When cranial ssuppressor removed three supervisorss dead. He takess hostage. Freess Perk and Agate. Hijack the frigate. Jettison hostagess inn space.'

'What else?'

He snarled in the Kitten's direction, thin lips curled around his thick jaws. The gold scales glittered brilliantly in the terrific sunshine. The dusty rags queued in an upward spiral when they reached the lip of the cenote. Each waited in turn under a black frame where two frocked assistants lifted their shirt fronts, exposing their flat bellies under the auspices of a scowling supervisor. One of the assistants held the ragged creature in check while the other planted a square nozzle extending from a waist high cylinder. After a grimace from the prisoner, a green spot lit on the top of the cylinder. When the nozzle was removed the restraining assistant fixed a staunch over the bleeding belly while the prisoner staggered towards the barracks.

He returned his hypnotic eye to her.

'Nothing you cannot digs for yoursselff.'

The Kitten's chest was within a whisker of his frontal plates. She placed her left claws close to her right shoulder, the pads facing out. He raised the baton. My hand felt for my disc.

'Now, then. What's all this, hm?'

A middle aged human carrying a white commpad crunched across the dry floor. He wore a genuine leather suit jacket and trousers; his frail head was topped with milky hair cut at sharp angles. He stopped within a shadow's length, a well practiced smile spread across his cheeks.

'We are investigating the escaped penitents. Who may I ask are you sir?'

'Professor Williams' he breathed through the smile.

He bowed to inspect the masses shuffling up the canyon stairways. One face among the filing heads dared glance up, the creased skin smothering an importuning eye pleading mercy.

The Sauroped pointed his baton and the terrestrial dropped to his knees. The Kitten's jaws opened in a silent hiss. The butt of his restraining device had the letters McB stamped on the handle.

'Mm Hm. Most unfortunate. The oblivious never find the road to redemption. Only by paying their debts can they hope for a sip of salvation.'

'What were your profit margins for the past month? What are they mining? Gold? Gemstones?' She looked ready to pounce on his back and sink her fangs in his neck.

The newcomer held his smile in place while my heart shattered. This feline compulsiveness had gone too far: Time to clip her claws. Before I could reproach her he replied brusquely, 'water.'

A thick shadow pooled around us.

'My dear Kitt, you have yet to earn any moral superiority over me.'

The shadow throbbed insipidly, the sound of a slowing engine.

'Now if you excuse me, we are rather busy, should you wish any further data please consult my general manager Mr. Ferguson.' He gestured with an open palm towards the descending airship; its shadow cast a wide spotlight shielding the hammering sun. I asked Spartacus to bring the skiff over. The Kitten was retracting and extending her claws while the Sauroped stubbed a sharp finger over the Cenote edge.

'He'ss not like them typical needy mammalss,' he sneered. Walks on two legss he doess. Now, you heard the masster.' He slowly emphasized those final words by imitating an adolescent who, from the paucity of their emotional puddle attempts to belittle the rational and lucid by talking in an inane and ponderous manner.

I though fuzzy face was about to perform the cleanest tracheotomy in history when her claws fully extended and her eyes threatened eternal damnation. Fortunately the Sauroped was called to demonstrate his talent with the baton and we were able to return to the skiff with our badges intact.

Mr. Ferguson's home was registered as a property outside Edinburgh, Scotland, a barren patch of leisure land north of England. It was turning into spring in this part of the world but it felt well below zero. We arrived at Ferguson's Baronial castle outside Edinburgh, four walls of rock that stood for thousands of years which probably had every modern convenience wired to the roof.

The banshee winds blew the straggly sandy grass flat as a tabletop and cleared the skies of any wisp if cloud. Daylight was fading when e announced our arrival before the studded wooden door, large enough to flatten the skiff. All the bleak windows were lifeless shadows. I shivered as the wind poked icy fingers between my collar; squeezing my bones stiff. I recalled in my studies of Europe how these isles were considered a temperate climate. Today the climate was in one hell of a bad temper.

'No one is home. Shall we wait or come back later? The Kitten was peering through a ground window at what seemed to be a bare kitchen.

'We'll come back later. We won't last a further minute out here.'

We walked to the skiff as twilight was passing. Between the blasted fields a glint of light appeared in a forest break some two hundred metres away. We watched the light flicker through the trees bending to the will of the howling wind, the branches black cracks against the gloomy sky.

Speechless, our eyes clicked with each other and crossed the field towards the spar of trees. The last light had vanished but we bore on nonetheless. The full moon was out anyway, offering some low radiance in this monochrome desolation. There was nothing around us but hedges, those trees and the castle. I became increasingly aware we were being watched, which grew stronger as we crossed the squelching ground. The sky night was a wonder of star constellations and the moon seemed lit by a billion watts. Halfway through the muck our boots slurping and burping in the ankle deep mud weighed half a tonnage each. I whined aloud, berating our rash decision, if there was any decision, to leave the skiff at the front gates.

Leaping over a shallow ditch I grabbed a rotting fence post and struggled through a thin hedge.

'Ow!'

'What?'

'Something bit me.' I don't know why I hushed my voice.

The Kitten, thanks to her feline vision, sailed over every clod and pitch hole underfoot. I held up my forefinger, dotted with a dark blob.

'It's a thorn, this is only a thorn bush,' she whispered on the other side of the fierce barrier, obviously planted to keep the barbaric hordes at bay.

The forest windbreak was roughly fifty metres wide. It was quite dark now so I crept, tentatively padding for twanging branches or ankle breaking animal holes. The Kitt strolled forward, completely at ease among the smothering branches, long grass, fallen trees and boulders. I allowed her to scout ahead.

We moved onto marshy ground as I pulled my foot free from a hungry pool. I lurched forward breaking my fall with my hands. The water was painfully cold, had seeped up my sleeves and now spilled over the lip of my boots and had instantly chilled my warm feet. The sooner we are issued with these new hydrotherm jackets the better I grumbled to myself. When I slithered to my feet the Kitt was gone.

'Lyrae?

'*Lyrae.*'

A screeching owl nearly induced a cardiac arrest. Quickly restoring my dislodged senses I glimpsed movement ahead. Before me, not fifteen metres distant, several shadows moved between the black trees.

'Ly-'

'Shh.'

Her warm palm covered my mouth. She pointed towards the shadows.

'Up there. Thirteen of them.'

'Who are they?'

'I don't know. They're on the move though.'

We crouched low. Me guessing and squirming my way through the dark forest, the Kitten slipping through the dark forest like a shadow herself. A light flashed up ahead. We crawled through tough grasses, stopping when we were ten metres or so from them. The smell of damp earth clung to my throat, rousing a sinking tiredness.

A group of cloaked figures were traversing the woods. The leader, carrying a single candle led a procession of somber shapes. The two at the rear carried a large bag, filled with something bulky which was tied to a pole which they shouldered between them. They trooped in single file with bowed heads, the hems of the cloaks stroking the patchy ground.

'Who?' I mouthed.

She shrugged, the laser intensity of her eyes following their path.

For a further minute we followed, cautiously. My stomach was playing up squeaking and gurgling in a call and response routine. *Oh, no you don't.*

They kept to a worn trail, each walking with considerate steps. When we ducked low in the grass they slowed to climb a slight incline. I rubbed my eyes, picking a crisp crumb from the corners. The entire scene was something out of an ancient film and would be if my hands weren't nipped a dozen times by stinging thistles and the cold didn't sap the living spirit from me. Any minute now and we'd hear a chorus of howls accompanied by thunder and lightning.

They eventually stopped, gathering in a wide circle. Thirteen in all, wearing identical midnight black cloaks, all human, six male, seven female. The candle was used to light pre-built firewood stacked in a high conical shape. Two men unclipped a portable table, assembling silver plates, knives, peculiar objects and figurines, a large bowl and two heavy ornate candlesticks which were placed on either end. When lit they revealed a long dagger resting on the plate baring unfamiliar carvings on the handle. We both lay there utterly fascinated and just a little apprehensive.

The men who fixed the table dragged the bag into the centre of the circle. By now each figure held a burning torch. They began to chant, a sonorous drone which encouraged the flames propped on top of their wooden handles to expand, throwing more light into the circle. We could see the half lit faces better, each ridge and hollow enhanced by the shade and light play.

The men struggled with the bag which was writhing in a noisy commotion. They cut the material carefully, releasing the thrashing lump inside. I peeped around the cloak closest to us and saw it was a fully grown ram, it jaws sealed by what looked like strong tape. The back legs were tied and it was hoisted above the ground, strung up on an overhead branch. The silver bowl was placed on the earth beneath it and the original leader picked up the blade. He stood beside the ram, raised his hands and began to mutter, then enunciate then cry:

'Hail Mars, blessed bringer of war!'

'Hail! Hail!' The circle intoned.

'Hail Ares, god of war!'

'Hail! Hail!'

He ran through a bewildering pantheon of military deities (some beyond even my fascinated studies of cults in the Denver library) the crowd repeating their salutations with each greeting. The ram struggled furiously, shaking the leaves of the tree. Although we were within the cover of scores of trees and low down, the sharp wind kept slicing my neck and hands, sanding my cheeks to a numbing discomfort. It was as if the wind was directed solely on me because neither the grass nor branches were moving. Above the chants I heard deep exhalations and occasional hissing, the way you constrict your throat muscles to release small wafers of carbon dioxide. I looked over my shoulder, certain we were being observed by a million malevolent eyes but there was nothing there except the outline of the forest standing in the eldritch light of the torches.

The man raised his knife, pressing the gleaming edge to the animal's throat. She shoved me in the ribs.

'We've got to stop this.'

I shifted on the cold earth, absolutely petrified yet icily compelled by the preposterous scene I was witness to. I don't think I could have stood even if there was a commendation at stake. I couldn't reply. My mouth was numb, my heart rate was in the hundreds and a chilling sweat crept along my back. Before I could turn to hush her she was up, wading into the group.

The chanting ceased.

The crowd erupted in a garbled protest.

'How dare you!' This is private land. Who are you?'

'I am sheriff Tcheetz. You are under arrest for the unauthorised attempted slaughter of restricted livestock.'

I watched, aghast.

The circle crowded her, furnishing weapons from the table, plates, bowls and candlesticks. They advanced on her, chanting unintelligible phrases. Two women lunged for her. In the soft firelight, the Kitten's claws were out. This had gone far enough. I plunged in.

'All right everyone, at ease. We are Syndicate sheriffs looking for a Mr. Ferguson: Lives in that nearby castle. Now, with your co-operation we can all resolve this matter.'

The knifeman took a pace before me. He was taller than he looked from our hidden cover. He pulled his hood down revealing his lean, grey face, tight lipped with a frail jaw. The swelling of Jowls were beginning in his cheeks and when he locked those stony eyes on me I involuntarily moved my left heel back.

'I am Mr. Ferguson. And who may I ask are you?'

'Sheriff Luten, 12th constellation, Associated Species Syndicate.'

The eyes remained steady, even his lips didn't move. His voice was the colour of those cold, dry eyes.

'If you are a sheriff then where may I ask is your identification?'

I instinctively reached for my chest, touching the empty square where my badge once sat. I spun around facing the route the Kitt and I stalked through. My torso was coated with cold mud mixed with leaves and grass.

'Oh, it must have fallen off while I was crawling through there.'

There was a fair amount of pushing and implied threats issued on both sides. We were reminded Syndicate law had no potency on Heraldic land. Three of the circle stepped back into the shelter of the shadow as Ferguson's face flushed with anger. We offered a hasty warning about animal welfare while we backed off through towards the tree line. The table and paraphernalia were packed away and the ram was untied. As I ripped the sleeve of my jacket climbing the fence I saw Ferguson's eyes roasting in the dying torchlight.

The Kitten and I slogged through the field back to the skiff; the moon beaming brightly upon us, the stars merrily twinkling in all their heavenly glory. I felt like the biggest ass in the galaxy.

Flying back across the Atlantic to interview the frigate crew, the Kitten sat beside me, trembling. She cleared her throat every few minutes then spat thick squirts overboard, wiped her lips then resumed that discreet, involuntary shivering. It wasn't until we sat with them in their food court did I realise my fists and teeth were clenched shut. For how long, I thought with hidden disquiet.

After being told nothing more from the frigate crew we couldn't have guessed ourselves we left Lennon 3, teaching escape velocity in under ten heartbeats, shooting towards L2 then rolling to the right, leveling off and heading into the outer depths, leaving the planets as specks of grit on the scanners. I tried to access the file on the Elyssian but was stumped by the persistent file not found message.

Before departure I bought a box of deli delight to settle my stomach. Within five minutes I'd emptied the box of two fried eggs, three pork sausages, four strips of bacon, a cup of beans and one slice of fried bread. While the last stub of sausage was worming down my gullet I tipped five sugars into the free cup of milky tea.

The Kitten sat quietly smoothing her mane. Her face snapped near my cheek.

'Where were you?

'Eh?'

'Back in Mexico?'

'What? Where do…what about your gross professional misconduct?'

'Don't quote meaningless guidelines to me.'

'One, I'm the overseer in this mission. Two, remember your place. '

'It's supposed to be a purgatory continent, not a slave mart.'

'It's not illegal. What you did was totally counterproductive.'

'Same old excuses, I can't believe we walked out of there with…the humiliation.'

'A little humility wouldn't go amiss.'

She busied herself with the communication console, sorting through various menus and folders, all the while making various hisses, chirrups, clicks and soft growls. She carried on like this before my huffiness gave way to molten impatience.

'What, what is it?'

She thumped her paw on the console's monitor.

'Either this piece of khak is defective or we're in the real shit.' I winced. If she swears once more…

A completely red screen flared up between us.

'I can locate the last co-ordinates of the frigate as it left the Lennon system but after that…It's like the entire ship has disappeared.'

I ran through the tracking procedure twice. The Kitten responded to my stupefied face.

'What are you thinking?'

I rubbed my chin with a free thumb.

'Well, as you say the ship either disappeared or...'

'Mm?'

'They've cleaned the banks; the banks, the chips, everything.'

I sat far back in my seat at an awkward angle.

'Who would have the skill or know how to wipe a Syndicate frigate?'

'There's only one planet stable enough to be entrusted with that level of knowledge.'

She continued tracking and scanning, probing the depths of the corvette's soul. With a harsh meow she switched off the screen. Her claws were extended beyond the edge of the arm rests. I conducted necessary searches, made myself look as if I was at best competent. Her irritation was unsettling me, coiling my muscles in tight cables and solidifying my stomach in a congealing snow pack. My brain was a flurry of letters trying to shape a few words to break the icy atmosphere between us. As I was about to ask if she wanted the thermostat adjusted she crossed her arms and sniffed.

'Some sheriffs we are. Where do we go from here?'

In answer to her question I sullenly programmed the co-ordinates for Elyssia.

Home.

Chapter 3

The Einstriv has a limited range and power capacity, requiring a recharge every six hours when travelling in Paraspace. We stopped at a medium moon sized service station after five hours of sedentary flight. The Kitten woke when the corvette moored and logged our arrival. We autodocked with the customary smooth entry and berthing procedure: I glanced towards her motionless profile as she yawned and stretched, her arms extending to nearly twice their length. She'd remained in the same posture during the blurred trip.

Passing the Portal Checks through the Syndicate entry we joined the mass of travelers.

'How did your last job go? She purred. We were entering the main concourse surging with people from distant galaxies, life forms and hybrid beings stopping over on long haul, deep space flights. I was stiff, hungry and trying to acclimatise to the myriad of perfumes and hot food, body odour and the white noise of over a thousand voices from the crypt like confines of the corvette. There is no training course for sitting still hour upon endless hour.

'All right. You?'

She looked up. 'Successful. Under supervision of course.'

We miraculously found an empty table. While she swatted plates, cups and wrappers into the mobile dumpster I gave our orders to the hovering drone. While we waited I jogged to the toilets. The sanitary facilities need to cater for every size and shape imaginable. The company who owned this particular station had installed a vast communal bowl. There were no racial, generic or gender distinctions. Everyone hoisted whatever exit channel they so possessed and let loose. There was however one private cubicle for the infirm and physically deprived/ I waited in line behind a short Qauug who insisted on rubbing his stumpy legs while talking to himself. I hope I never embarrass myself like that. During the wait my bowls protested noisily, a wholesale riot was in progress. Week-long civic unrest with fully armed pacifier squads quelling ranks of flamethrowers and biotoxic bombs. Soon I was bending over, joining the Qauug in enthusiastic leg rubbings. When it was his turn he took an eternity. When I finally was relieved I nearly broke the pan in thunderous appreciation. I carefully walked back to the food court, careful not to disturb the frying disc between my legs.

On my return at least the food was served.

'You took your time!'

 She was nibbling a raw feche. I sat down, scooping mouthfuls of mixed meat from my deep plate. I ignored her remark, chomping hard on my succulent cubes of roast torcin and vaco. Her almond eyes rolled from side to side. Behind me, a table of privateers or mercenary types guffawed, slamming their table as they shouted insults to other diners.

'Good, yeah, snared a couple of Engele smugglers. You what? Haw, haw, haw.'

Among the various skin gland secretions, fat and pheromone, bacteria and hormonal fog there was a strong hydrocarbon lingering in the busy atmosphere. I opened my nostril a fraction, filtering the multitude of odours. That heavy stench was increasing. Something foul and filthy was in the air.

The Kitten scanned the canteen with slow eyes.

'You'll use up all your lives eating that stuff.'

Right. That's it.

I laid my hands on the table, now turning a shade of sapphire. I was still gripping my cutlery.

48

'I can't afford to eat healthy, as you'll soon discover,' I warned, holding my wrist slightly raised so the tip pointed towards her face.

I swallowed the last spoonful without chewing.

A distinct smash from the mercenaries table interrupted my admonitions.

The Kitten adjusted her posture arched her back before leaning over my plate. She spoke between locked jaws without removing her frown from my shoulder.

'Rhyddian Kli is sitting with those bounty hunters.'

Ryhddian Kli. Three metres tall, a dangerously psychotic killer - wanted for the murder of Sheriff Lo S.

'Not our problem.'

'We can do him, here, now.'

'Look,' I whispered, 'this isn't within our remit. We'll call the nearest office and arrange the pickup. We're on the trail of three dangerous fugitives, we can't compromise the objectives.'

'Compromise yourself. I'm going to swipe him.'

I heard Kli cackling above and behind my head. Our blue and yellow uniforms stood out like a Madonna 6 moon. His nerves were either dead or his brain was sleeping or he simply didn't care two khaks about our presence.

The fur crowning the Kitten's frown was bristling; her eyes looked possessed of some maniacal spirit.

'We need to follow procedure, adhere to protocol, follow the appropriate strategy,'

'We don't need that rubbish now,' she hissed, nodding over my shoulder.

I turned to witness two local sheriffs approach the table. Young humans, who by their stance and demeanour looked freshly processed. The mercenaries fell into a sudden hush. The Kitten removed the disc from her belt. My guts froze, my muscles coiled, I tried to regulate my breathing through my nostril.

'Rhyddian Kli, you are charged under directive 1.34 for the murder of-

I didn't hear the remainder of the arrest statement nor recognize the arresting sheriff. There are ten thousand of us scattered across the galaxy really. You never meet or work with more than three or four hundred throughout your career.

The noise in our section of the canteen dimmed to a few rattles and taps punctuated by snatched whispers. I would have to intervene. These were green shoots, dealing with some pretty rotten fruit. A pair of furtive shadows left the room, skipping for the exit. I'd seen that shape before…perhaps the Savoy?

The mercenaries continued eating, showing little concern for the arresting officers. I heard a glass slide off the table followed by defiant gulps. Someone broke wind and was applauded. Do I let them handle this? Remembering the farce with Williams and Ferguson, my guts tricked into cold burns.

The sheriff repeated his order. The Kitten shrunk her shoulders and head concealing the disc beneath the table.

-you either come with us willingly or we will be forced to…'

The table took off, breaking in two as the halves were tossed into the humming air. Screams, shrieks, squeaks, roars and hisses erupted, converting the tense lull in the room into a cacophony of panic. By the time I turned and removed my disc the Kitten pounced.

Kli had already pierced his index spike through the throat of the arresting officer. While his other limb plated in shining velcour, deflected his partner's first shot, the nearest bounty hunter to me had collapsed at my feet, his face ploughed with glistening red furrows from the Kitt's blow. I stunned the second hunter with an incapacitating neural shot. He reeled, drawing his weapon.

Kon!

I forgot that Riglensz have two nervous systems, direct and alternating.

The second blast hit the wrist bearing his Thermox pistol. There wasn't time for a follow up so I wrapped my rubbery arm under his elbow joint, held him in an arm lock and struck two sharp strikes on his double plexus. He slumped, a moan of extirpation gargling from his chest.

The Kitten was tangling with the final bounty hunter in deadly claw to claw combat.

Her opponent was a humanoid cyborg, armed with a gleaming blade the size of his forearm, now whistling through clean air. The Kitt dodged and parried the blows easily. However, Kli had ripped the other sheriff in half and was striding towards her. I aimed a mortal beam of ion shot into his bony sternum. He stopped, checked his chest was still in one piece in a puzzled glare then spotted me holding my disc as if my Esocard was refused credit. In one leap he towered above me, the stink of his burnt scales clouding the invaluable space between us.

Before his first swing even gathered momentum I was rolling clear. I knew that would be his opening move. The canteen emptied at full pelt with diners either retreating to their ships or flattening themselves against the far wall for a reasonably safe view of the unfolding chaos.

Kli kicked out his snapping feet, smashing an adjacent table, wrecking benches into jagged pieces. I tried another shot, this time for his horned head and quivering pincers. The blast knocked one of the horns clean from his hairless scalp. Now he was annoyed.

He unleashed a deafening screech which cleared the few spectators left against the wall. Before I could recover my stunned senses he had me pinned to the floor, lowering his head until I saw my oval face and thin lips reflected in his obsidian eyes.

Enclosing my face in his serrated claws, the canteen zeroed to a narrow hole in a creeping tunnel. My eyes stung, his weight was crushing my lithe body. I screamed and struggled to the point of exhaustion. The strength holding me down was appalling. Warm fluid gushed into my eye sockets. I was going under, sucked into luminal space-time.

Then the encompassing darkness retreated. My vision returned to an opalescent blur. Steady eyes were scrutinizing me. I fought to stand but the force held me firm.

'Luten?'

I filled my lungs with hearty air, drew it deep to awaken my reserves of Kon.

'Luten?'

The Kitten's chocolate fudge voice.

The pressure eased as furry hands helped me to my feet. When I cleared my eyes the hazy figure of Kli came into focus.

'You good?'

I placed my hand on her bony shoulders.

'What happened?'

I tried to monitor and assess the carnage we stood in.

'It's fine; Kli's dead.'

Lying splayed on top of broken tables, squashed food and streaks of blood was Kli, black eyes replaced by two yellow swampy holes.

Her claws were coated in the same yellow juice.

'You all right?'

I turned to face my partner. Her fur was slick with three different varieties of bodily fluids. Her eyes remained the same: Clear lime, focused, feline.

I wiped my face, my lips, cleaned the sloppy stuff from my caked uniform. Hard to believe that thing was once from the same embryos I was plastered in two days ago.

'Yeah, yes, thanks. Thank you, Lyrae.'

She placed one hand on top of the other between her knees.

'My pleasure,' she purred.

Chapter 4

By the time the anarchy in the spaceport was probed, processed and purified by a delegation of local sheriffs we were on our second Paraspace route and I had changed into a fresh uniform kept in the corvette's hold. I kept my own soft undervest on. The irritating regulation garments usually turned my silken body into a skin of rashes.

We arranged our sleep in shifts for the next twelve hours. I sunk into a marshy indulgence before going under. When I woke Lyrae was pulling towards one of our outer moons. Elyssia is an independently governed planet even though she is within the Association administration. There is nothing to export save the character of its people. The planet was chosen as the caretaker of security programs for Syndicate ships because of her neutrality and subjective stance in all Association affairs.

We flew in a preliminary entry course into Elyssia's spatial rings: The excruciatingly ponderous orbit and torturous, grinding spin already fibrillating my sphincter. My upper arms were stiff and the recurring twitch under my eye trembled.

The corvette entered her atmosphere on auto, gliding towards the surface. The twitch ballooned into a spasm. Declaring our intent and purpose to the gatekeepers residing in the Fennile mountain range we powered forth. The familiar pink Olepha Sea with its white archipelago islands rising in ragged pilgrimage to the shore crinkled my eyes. I spent a happy time there in my infancy. A sleek cephal leapt from the churning waves, twisted its oblong body then flipped broad fins before crashing beneath the surface.

Lyrae followed the creature's acrobatics with unerring sight.

'Meow.'

I showed her the green mountains whose turquoise forests were alive with birds of every hue, beak and wingspan. We cruised over the numerous communes and settlements, the buildings all hugging and holding or snuggling into hills, rivers and meadow. A pyramid might have a base melting into boulderfields. Domes and spheres undulate over grassy slopes and octagonal edifices erupt from sheer cliffs. Our sun flowered scarlet and peach as it stuck to the clean sky like a chemical stain.

A tawny haired concierge greeted us at the port all smiles and sweet salutations. She practically climbed in beside us into the passenger seat of the hovercraft, asking if here any further service she could provide. Only when the craft was airborne did my twitch cease.

The brief flight to my parents took us over the water gardens where we plopped the hovercraft in the vehicle arena. The two minute walk revealed to Lyrae the maem flowers chiming whenever she passed her hand over the bobbing petals.

'This place is amazing,' she remarked.

I sighed. 'Yes, it is pretty neat I suppose.'

Traversing the tessellated concourse to my parent's triple domed house was accompanied by harmonious music drifting from the flanking streams. The door was open but no one was home.

'Must be out.'

Lyrae was admiring a ceramic bowl painted with wavy lines. The orange fruits shone brilliantly in the sunshine making them look like holograms.

I'll show you around if you like.'

'Mmm.'

She was so stuck on that bowl, I wasn't sure she heard. I stepped closer.

'That's a 3000.5 cycle meditation bowl. Belonged to our ancestors.'

'Beautiful.'

'There's nothing but beauty here,' I mumbled to myself.

We strolled down an avenue of conical trees. 'In high summer if you sit here long enough you can hear them sing the frequency of your soul.' She turned to me with that default smile, thin and precise.

I guided her around the Zsush falls where after a hard day's contemplation you could lie in the clear blue waters on a bed of lilies and allow the vibrant crystals to soothe your nerves.

'So quiet, so still.'

Something which terrified me from epiglottis to bile duct but I wasn't going to tell her that.

We passed a circle of women dressed in white robes chanting Kon's name in a repetitive monotone. Clutches of poets lay buried in humming meadows awaiting their muses, a painter finished her still life as a bard strummed by and three dancers rehearsed their forthcoming performance in the local amphitheatre. Before we returned to my parents we sat beside the cascades, a wide cliff veined with turquoise where the white waterfalls surges from the Ano River, crashing in a magical burst of spray on flat rocks. Some children were capering in the shallow pools. Violet and gold flowers filled the banks spreading an uplifting smell of joy around us. Lyrae lay on her back absorbing the benevolent warmth of our sun.

'This place is-'

'Yeah. Come on let's get back.'

We returned through the Falla, a valley filled with furry leaved plants. Lyrae held her hand out deep in the petals, caressing each delicate flower as she passed. With each touch they bloomed, producing a ripe peach. Lyrae asked for permission to pick one so she gently plucked the heavy fruit. I rolled my eyes, refusing a bite when she offered.

 We were only several footsteps from the open archway of my parents' when my father emerged within the portal dressed in his customary white robes.

'Welcome home, beloved.'

My mother greeted me likewise and I introduced Lyrae and we all embraced and they offered blessings 'within and around you' and them my stomach squirmed.

A light supper was arranged on a low table glittering with crystalline flecks. Lyrae studied the abstracts placed on the walls, the neo-philamena pottery and hanging woven tapestries. We sat opposite my father and mother who sat with majestic grace on cushioned mats.

'It warms my heart to see you again, my son.'

'Likewise, father.'

He showed me his palm in the traditional exchange of Kon. We touched skin. Then my mother and I did the same. Then the repeated the whole procedure with Lyrae.

I wagered she was lapping this right up. We ate raw garkweed which tastes as appetising as it sounds. Lyrae stared forlornly at her plate, nibbling the tough fibres which gave me an esoteric delight.

When the plates and cutlery was cleared we convened to the heart space with steaming bowls of stran, green tea which tastes worse than salty coffee. We at in quiet appreciating until cool tiredness arrived. My mother lit incense and candles while my father arranged soft cushions. He operated the shutters which withheld even the thinnest thread of light. Paperback tomes on thought healing and emotional growth packed the shelves. Some musical instruments were gathered in a corner. Stone sculptures stood against the circular wall encircling a clear crystal the size of my head.

I opened the dialogue with the usual Elyssian preamble.

'Father, I truly wish in my heart I could remain in your beloved company with blessed mother. However, I come on official Association matters. A few...one of our days has passed since three terrorists broke out of a purgatory facility on Lennon 3. They have hijacked a Syndicate frigate and disappeared. I believe they have erased the ships memory and signature programs. One of the fugitives is an Elyssian.

My parents sat expressionless, nodding in appropriation as they moved their hands in gentle gestures. I heard Lyrae purring with satisfaction.

'I need to know what I'm up against. Firstly, who this Elyssan could be, second, how could they have gained access to erase an entire frigate's memory?'

My father closed his emerald eyes, lowered his head and breathed audibly, deeply, slowly. Rising to the window he stood facing a bridge of stars crossing the velvet night sky on the shutter's hologram.

'Search your own heart my son,' he told the 3t- cluster.

The candles flickered briefly. The head sized crystal clouded. We sat in the circle sipping our bitter green.

'My only regret in my life is your stay on earth. You missed the crucial hypothalamus reconfiguration...the burden I must bear until we shed this skin and return to Kon.'

A rumbling broke from my throat as if I was hawking up phlegm.

'Not this dead wood again.'

He returned to his place on the cushion. My mother's chin touched her chest, her hands clasped in a loose gesture of prayer.

'You should have joined me in the diplomatic team, instead you fly off to prove yourself a, a what, my son? I mean no disrespect Lyrae.' he added as a rejoinder to the tiresome reunion.

I'd endured this too many times. His culpability for my biological survival instincts being allowed free ride over my higher thinking, being allowed to flourish, weakening my connection to Kon, my telepathic abilities warped into an ego trip.

'Look father, this runaway, he's killed three guards and two prisoners and Kon knows how many crew on the frigate. What Elyssian could do this?'

My father unwrapped his legs from the seated posture, stretching before raising his arms. When he returned to his position he spoke deliberately.

'Telepathic powers are highly discouraged. Not only do they disrupt the continuum and atomic equanimity, they are a flagrant and shameless flaunting of the puppet self.'

He tapped his head.

'Would such an Elyssian exist he was kept well hidden from us or...'

'Or what?' I stooped in close for this one.

'Or he was raised on another system.'

Lyrae and I slept in my old room, she on the aerobed I on a raft of mats and cushions. I listened to the warbling mud insects, the songs which used to help me drift off into dream worlds of dogfights and Paraspace journeys to undiscovered worlds. Today they simply kept me awake.

My Sondisc flashed steadily. I opened the in tray to find three texts downloaded. They were gifts from my grandfather on my first birthday. He was a consultant for Pulsar Networks. He thought they would inspire me to greatness. 'Be the best: Avatarhood in a day' by W. Shakespeare, 'Becoming Excellence' by C. Dickens and 'How to crush opposition effortlessly' by W. Blake had sat in my resource pod unopened for eight lonely years.

'Psss.'

The outline of Lyrae's head protruded from the edge of the bed.

'Yeah?'

Where would you go if you were on the run? I mean, what would be the safest part of the galaxy to hide from Syndicate presence? '

I dunno. Not many places a Syndicate frigate could be concealed. Of course, if you delete the insignia and markings I suppose...'

'The Glitter system?'

'Possibly. Though there would be a lot of snitches who'd inform on you for a few Kronium bars.'

'Would have to be the back of beyond, really.'

I was sitting up, dressed in my father's spare tunic cross legged.

'True.'

Lyrae eased herself off the bed. She booted up her disc. The glow cast furtive shadows on the walls.

'Still can't locate the file of the Elyssian.'

After sorting through more submenus she returned to the main contents, opting for star system navigation. She projected a holographic image of local star systems linked with a subscreen of the wider galaxy.

'They'd need a pretty airtight refuge.'

She sorted through local hotspots and hideouts, pirate routes and abandoned shipping lanes. Entering several more variables and adjusting the parameters she waited for the discs assessment. Three results flashed before our eyes.

'There!' she announced. Before our pale faces lit by the holograms light, Lyrae's claw underlined the bottom option.

'Sagittarius?' I queried.

'Yuss. Only a complete fool would go there.'

'Yeah,' I countered, 'or a complete madman.'

Chapter 5

While Lyrae was having breakfast with my parents I took a walk to my brother's holomemorial, placed beside the pond at the foot of the garden. His image stood, life sized. The holomemorial aged chronologically: He was now a fully grown ten year old adult. We lost him when he was only a year in a pirate ambush when he was returning with my father from a diplomatic counsel in a recent area of de-confliction. As their unarmed and unescorted transport was about to make the Paraspace launch, the pirates struck. Before the jump a ship is at its most vulnerable as scanners and shields divert power while the Einstriv boots up the entry co-ordinates.

The pirates froze the oscillation chip, isolating the transport without an escape route. As the shields were also lowered they boarded easily. They were a mixed crew of humanoids who grabbed everything worth a single credit and hauled the crew and passenger onboard their surrounding vessels. When a human fitted with a heart modulator pulled my brother to his feet by the hair my father, unused to the outrageous violation of his personal and senatorial position tried to punch him, he was knocked out before his fingers tightened.

He regained consciousness on board a salvage cruiser who assured him over the following days he was the only survivor on board his ship. My father sold a many family assets and took two years leave to search for his lost son, eventually arriving back on Elyssia greyer than I remembered him.

I marveled at the astonishing resemblance to my sibling. The arching forehead, the eyes cut to a hard slope from the brows, the tapering jaw. I could have been gazing at myself in my own cubicle holomirror.

'It's remarkable isn't it?'

'Mother! I didn't hear you approach.'

She was dressed in a shiny robe, so refined it flowed from her limbs like her long hair lifting in the breeze. She held my waist as we both bowed our heads in unspoken homage to our beloved kin.

'Wyken would have been proud of you,' she exclaimed. Her voice was naturally soft and felicitously reassuring. We walked arm in arm up the smooth pebbled path to the house.

'A pity father doesn't feel the same.'

Her arm squeezed mine. 'He carries much regret.'

'Resentment is more like it.'

'Your bickering weakens me Luten, why must it be so? When you are gone all he talks about is you, the fond memories you share, the times ahead when you both age, when you will return.'

I poisoned my feet attentively on the white stones, operating at half the speed I usually took when walking. My head rotated, absorbing the multisensory arrangement of raucous flowers, listening to a flock of winged aphens sitting in the branches of a tree. I stopped before we arrived at the rear entry.

'Mother, I...I...'

'I know. Luten, I love you too. You are changing, change brings instability, with instability comes change. Find the inner sense which sustains you.'

She held my cheeks in delicate hands, her ultraviolet eyes a coruscating feeling I turned from, walking into the vapid house alone, I called for Lyrae and we took off with prolonged thanks and obligatory departing customs.

Lyrae cleared the Yungus Ridge by the space between her whiskers, banking the hovercraft in a sharp left towards the Ine Valley. I shuddered involuntarily.

When I returned from Lennon 3 I had a roaring argument with my father. He insisted I undergo the purification ceremony. Carrying a pit filled with dense despair I left home that night, sleeping on the ridge without a bite to eat or an inkling of where I was going or what I would do. A flurry of giggles helped me surface from a solid sleep.

Three girls stood over me. They were throwing little twigs and flowers on my face. The shortest, wearing a loose band around her brilliant red hair nudged my toe. They were free seekers: Drop outs, soul searchers, slackers and time wasters, living on generous donations and the good air of Elyssia. I snuggled right in.

They were tolerated and in some circles, encouraged. I bounced between the red head and her pals, getting high on wron stalks and fleeting trysts. Generally having a good old time, as was my constitutional right, but three months into her pregnancy I fled, taking what few belongings were slung over my shoulder and enrolled in the Academy the following moon cycle. Annoying habits became fuming arguments, arguments erupted into pitched battles. During one particularly bilious debate on my fidelities she burned my satchel holding every precious hard drive, item of clothing and to my shame, Hank's old sheriff badge. The following weeks were attritional. I held my position until, in an intoxicated fit she implied by tautological allegory the baby might not be ours.

The Academy interview was easy. I just had to lie that I was better than all the rest of the five hundred applicants squeezed into the training wing's combat simulation arena.

When I was only three full cycles all I wanted was to fall in love, marry; father some offspring. Following one botched relationship after another, chasing lost causes and running from pursuing disasters: My honey heart curdled to sour cream.

The outskirts of Elrah with its banks of sunburst lilies, marble archways and approaching vista of domes, pyramids and needling towers rising through the clouds was flush with hovercraft. We joined the wide flowing channels through the low roofed homes embedded with cherished gardens. I pointed out a few areas of interest, some fountains and art monuments. Gathered in the park, scores of Elyssian children enjoyed their al fresco lessons, in some cases with two teachers per pupil.

Wide channels separated the buildings and as the suns were at full seasonal warmth we parked up and walked to the central hall of records. Some of the passing pedestrians giggled at my uniform while most bowed or greeted Lyrae with a 'good morning' or open handed gesture.

We alighted on the aerovator, an ascending column of jet air which waited until we stepped off onto the second floor of the Hall before receding back to the ground. The floor was filled with large leafed plants and water effects while the latest composition by Noryn rippled from the speakers. A wooden hand carved sign bearing the record facilitator's name was placed casually on his desk. He raised his head when he heard us approach.

'Ah, Luten, most benevolent greetings to you, my brother.'

We repeated the same rigmarole as last night when Lyrae met my parents.

After I gave the fugitive's name he inserted a crimson disc into an oval console, immediately casting a holograph of multiple grids and panels. Each of us has our own unique moniker, as you probably surmised.

After a brief pause the blank screen was accompanied by the console stating 'no search results found'. He repeated the request, which only resulted in a quicker response. After feeding his holoimage and inputting manual data and profile specs the facilitator shook his head, spreading his arms and finally after three more attempts, fudging and twiddling he conceded defeat. We left him behind the holograph, alone and on the brink of unshed tears.

On the fourth floor we were assured by an overly anxious support assistant that under no circumstance, context or wherewithal could any life form, species or sentient being access the codes to erase or modify a ship's primary programming and datastore. Besides the master chips were transferred to Jagger 2 and we disposed of open-source ages ago didn't we read the memo?

Lyrae and I swapped looks sheepishly.

As the aerovator placed us lovingly on the fragrant walkway Lyrae suggested my father had been correct in his assumption the fugitive must have been born and raised elsewhere.

'Well,' I sang as we returned to the hovercraft, 'looks like a long haul into the back of beyond.'

Lyrae smoothed her ears with the back of her hand. She stroked hair under her chin then inspected the tip of a fore claw.

'Yuss.' She pulled an invisible piece of dirt from the claw before spitting it on the pristine walk way to the aghast of passersby. 'Looks like a long ride ahead of us partner.'

It doesn't matter if you're carried on the back of a rainbow unicorns while drunk on red lily juice while every muscle is massaged in flurease oil; long haul travel is a pain in the hole.

When the Einstriv engages the field oscillation plates and the corvette shimmers through Paraspace and you enter Kon time your bottom grows numb on the padded seat while your thighs twitch you wish there was some more convenient method of inter stellar travel.

The whirling light before us was the only mutual distraction inside the cabin. Two successive green flashes on the panel suggested we had two more hours left to endure. Lyrae sat half curled, the warm purrs the sole evidence she was still alive. She hardly spoke tow words to my parents leaving with a tight smile, the default position of her mouth and a raised pad. My mother kissed both my tight cheeks, longer than she usually did. My father exercised his annual cautionary tale which I conveniently forgot

While we waited beside the cooing plants and suffered Noryn's greatest hits in the port lounge with the suffocating scent of bern flower essence Lyrae landed her paw on my shoulder as I waved away the third concerned face asking if we needed a complimentary massage.

'How you doing?'

I turned, frowning. 'Fine, I'm good.'

'You don't look it,'

'I'm all right.' She removed the hand, leaned on the back of her chair and hooked her fingers.

'If you want to talk about your mum and dad...'

In one uninterrupted move I sat upright while sliding away from her mewling. Inside my head the demonic scream of an Einstriv flew from ear to ear.

'No, actually, no I don't. The bern flower stench was choking my throat. I wanted nothing more to take a shot with an ion carbine at the sickly mush spewing from the loudspeaker.

She rested her warm pad on my back then returned to her disc. 'I'm sorry.'

Thank Kon a caressing voice declared our corvette was ready between the infernal racket and cloying air.

At last we were off shooting for the delights of free flight.

Then we ground to a decisive stop behind a rumbling queue of personnel transporters.

'Get a bloody move on!' I howled.

Lyrae sat through my impassioned rant about the nuisance of public transport and how I'd ban all these infuriating space hogs.

'It's enough to give you homesick blues,' I snarled to no one in particular.

Chapter 6

As we rippled through Paraspace the bern essence still clung to my skin, uniform and hair. The morning birdsong, mmnbora blossom and splashing fountain water cooling my throbbing feet seemed to return the further we left Elyssia behind. I shuddered, pushing these sentimental trivialities aside.

The corvette kept us abreast of diagnostics updates between requests for hot drinks and snacks. I wasn't keen on eating a standard meal. In fact I desired nothing more than to crawl inside the hold and wallow in the dark. I tried to calculate arrival times and alternate leads we could pursue. My parent's recent scent and facial expressions were imprinted vividly from that visit. A sinkhole was dragging my thoughts deeper into a tailspin and I found it an increasing struggle to concentrate on matters at hand. I tried to recall the vague memories of that ethereal summer, free from mindless duty and the 'greater responsibility' inherent in my father's weekly sermons. In a heavy mood I remembered the morning after I lost my virginity and the overwhelming anti climax it was after all the fanfare among my human coevals in Colorado. Our next plasmoball fixture was also nipping at my nerves so I unclipped the Sondisc and powered up.

I found a sports channel and caught up with the latest results. The Sondisc wasn't able to pick up a clear transmission so I used the corvette's comms. Oh joy! The enemy, Obsemouri, dropped points against the third placed team, although it looked as if they were given every decision in their favour according to the stat chart. Gracemon were still playing the last few minutes, holding on to a 1-0 advantage. Lyrae was twitching her whiskers about something or other.

'Yes, mh hm.'

They've been given a last gasp infringement! We were nowhere near the attacker!

'So you're fine with that?'

'Yeeeeeeeeeeeeeeeeeessssssssssssssssss!' I screamed.

Saved, saved, saved, we are on equal points, this could go down to one of the biggest playoffs in history.

'All right, sheez.' She opened a tube of dried feche and chewed her way through half a bar.

I checked the Elyssians file for the hundredth time. Corrupted or missing. Something smelt distinctly fishy.

Chapter 7

I was still grinning like the holographic model above my apartment block when we returned to visible space some distance from Jagger. The green, brown and blue world never looked so beautiful.

'This is where I'm going to retire.'

Three enormous conduction globes shone, brighter than Jagger, EM inductors splicing power to nine lower globes in turn distributing energy to twenty seven sub globes before converting electricity to every home, street and city. Jagger 2's cool atmospheric aura welcomed us and during our descent saw the magnificent cities spread every inch of Zaxx, the only continent whose ellipses, trapeziums and diamonds covered the island splurge floating on the overwhelming ocean planet. I kept the corvette on manual, steering us into the Association base. Jagger 2 had the thinnest Syndicate presence of any biosphere.

'You've been here before?'

I smiled.

'No. Well, only in vidshows or simulations.'

'Hm.'

'No interfering do-gooders telling you what and what not to eat, to fly, to buy. Unlimited opportunities, everyone free from those horrendous restrictions, everyone free to follow their dreams.'

'Right.'

Instead of the usual separate Syndicate and Civilian portals, we found ourselves standing in a queue with the other mortals with the free runners, the merchants and assorted riff raff.

A deadpan employee of the Stellaport stood sharply in a black tunic.

'Corporate title.'

'Ahh, sorry?'

'Certificate number then.'

'I do apologise for my-'

'Your name!'

'Oh. Luten, this is-'

He threw a mercurial glance at my partner.

'I didn't ask her name did I? If I wanted her name I would ask her wouldn't I?'

I shook my head, covered the space where my badge sat with tight fingers and shuffled behind the queue waiting for Lyrae on the other side.

After log in we made an appointment with a high official. He lived in a residential rhombus in the Zaxx land mass on top of a massive plateau wreathed in impenetrable jungle. We took a skiff, gliding through the swarming craft and bodyboards which seemed to take no observance of our position or flight route. Climbing above the garish spires and spinal citadels we swerved to avoid a couple of ships roaring beside us like stray missiles from below as they tore into the clouds. The Stellaport and the surrounding conurbation was a mess of noise, a scramble of activity, flashing lights, and frenetic traffic. Clearing the urban morass we headed for the coast, following the skiff's recommend course.

Flying over a spectacular retail reservation, I pointed out the ingenious cost efficiency of the buildings, especially a holoplatform store which was simply four poles forming a square. The shop was perennially open so there was no need for roofs or doors or walls. Although a pack of security droid hovered discretely out of sight, ready to deliver an electroshot to any furtive thief. Like all the urbanized sectors there was a steady stream of cascading consumers.

'Fff, doesn't anyone work around here?'

I sniggered long and loud.

'That's the beauty of this place. It works. You see Lyrae, everything is met with fully eased reliance. Your needs are satisfied, everyone is happy because of meticulous customer care. Life keeps moving, delivery of product is the only constant in the volatile worlds, therefore, maintains a harmonious equilibrium of supply. Keep them busy and you keep them clean.'

'Why are they predominantly human?'

I cleared my throat. 'Well, significant numbers couldn't handle the overwhelming information overload these last few hundred years. They see this planet as a sanctuary,'

'Too many minds blown.'

'Possibly.'

'What an upside down world.'

'Good job our brains correct the inverted visual data then isn't it?'

'It's only that way to make it fit with what we already know, Luten.'

I let that one pass.

We passed a coastline of vermillion cliff where a pack of enormous construction vehicles were devouring the land. One or two huge jawed excavators were chomping through the cliff while gigantic cranes scooped the material into the skips of transports with tracks the length of a medium sized destroyer.

As we skimmed the surface of the sea we spotted Zaxx in the distance. We flew over hundreds of small artificial islands where private villas, castles and palaces were crowned on hills surrounded by carefully assorted trees and shrubs. One of them was provisionally booked in my name. I'd made a good profit on the apartment, enough for a deposit. The plateau rose from the jungle, a titanic slab dominating the horizon. Bordering Zaxx were beaches on par with Mexico. As we trimmed the tree tops all we saw was the dark green canopy. There was no evidence of habitation, nor any animal to see.

'Here's the example of consummate self realization. He starts out with nothing, works day and night to build his career, his own business then an empire. He's on the board of a score of companies, has given advice to presidents, generals and chiefs and is part of every major policy and decision in the Syndicate. His place is well earned, believe me.'

She coughed; a ragged hawking.

'That's not what I read.'

'Oh?'

'Seems he was handed a fortune on his twenty first birthday. Blew the lot on a dead horse and nearly bankrupted his family estate. Thanks to some rich dirt he holds on an old school chum, he bullied and bribed his way to the top.'

'You mustn't read everything you believe.'

The skiff climbed around the plateau in spirals so we could savour the view of the lush greenery, spotting a series of staged waterfalls which shouldered the Xcetle River as it wove towards the sea.

'I can see why you want to retire here,' Lyrae remarked.

On the roof of the plateau we sailed towards a gorgeous walled estate. Breathtaking sunken gardens guarded by gold statues stood in silent observation. The main house was a three storey mansion, displaying the most exquisite architecture I had seen outside England.

The consultant was waiting for us, seated beside his pool. We joined him and accepted his offer of drinks. Well, I did, Lyrae declined because Lactodrene wasn't a popular beverage in these parts. We asked about the possibility of any unauthorized personnel gaining access to the procedures and practices of resetting a frigate's databanks and were given an affirmative negative.

'The information is three levels above top secret. So class...hhmm, ahmm...excuse me...so classified in fact, our screening pro...' He coughed, great spluttering and gasping fits. Lyrae and I jumped to our feet, reaching for our miniature medikits. He raised a shaky hand. Racing from thin air an android sped to his side, inserting a shiny tube into his slavering mouth. It looked like a P2 dispenser, medication we administer to criminals to control impulsivity. Those who don't respond positively are sent to purgatory colonies, like the one on Lennon 3. His flushed cheeks regained their cool pallor. Wiping his lips he continued.

'No. we employ only the select few, those with the requisite breeding and worthwhile background to befit the responsibility of data ownership One requires the most advantageous stock in the race. Besides, any alien presence would be immediately tracked and appropriately managed.'

Every follicle within my skin stood to attention. My face felt thick with cold grease and I had a compelling urge to scratch my head. We were dismissed as glibly as the penitentiary owner in Mexico. I carried a molten rock in the pit of my stomach. On our return to the skiff, Lyrae reached up to dip her fingertips in the smoky clouds drifting overhead, tittering when the clouds parted to swim past her hands. The journey to the foot of the plateau was swift: The return to the mainland even quicker.

'What was all that about?'

I moved my head slightly left to right, 'I dunno.'

'Does this shit happen often?'

A flock of seabirds strafed a shoal of fish. The waves climbed high, spraying us when the water hit the side of the skiff.

I don't know...I don't usually deal with people like that.'

She had that possessed countenance, eyes wide, moving sensually to the rail. She was following the fin of a large fish.

'Well, he seemed like a complete mutt to me,'

When the fin slipped under the waves she joined me at the helm, standing comfortably close. As we arrived on shore, landing near the Stellaport, she leapt from the skiff, allowing a cold draught to blow the heat she left on my bicep,

We stretched our legs, taking a walk through the busy city centre of Vantresh. I smiled and nodded to parading pedestrians who either ignored my salutations or hastily turned away, as if we were a pair of Giggesthens. The swollen chests of men and women pushed past us. They wore freshly bought clothes they would discard tomorrow according to the live commercials. Some androids skipped beside the pedestrians, supplying them with a steady stream of food, drinks and compliments on their choice off dazzling attire. The magnatheric freepath running the middle of each pavement conveyed stern marketing and advertising types flash past, buoyant on gaseous cushions, they looked as if they were seated on invisible chairs. A family of six meroids flowed near us, slouched in a tangled bush of arms and legs. Flashy skiffs swarmed around our heads. We had to duck to occasionally avoid having our heads snapped from our shoulders.

Thousands of black specks stormed around us.

'Where have all these flies come from?' Lyrae growled. Swatting a handful from her face,

'Oh, they aren't insects I retorted.

'No?'

'No, everyone is assigned their own personal monitoring drone.'

The crowd like shoals or flocks stopped instantly, pausing in one unified move. Some commotion ahead was gathering a great deal of excitement. Children were hoisted on shoulder, the slender were ruffled back. Lyrae and I barged through to inspect the curious kerfuffle. People were lining each side of the road, the cheering and screams were painful on the ears. Even Lyrae flattened hers to cover the cacophony. From a bend up ahead, thousands of colourful ribbons and scraps of tissue were billowing in a storm, carpeting the street and heads of those gathered. A magnaband was bunching us into the walkway, preventing any intrusion on the road but also squashing us against each other. If this continues any longer, we'll have to intervene I thought.

Trundling around the bend an articulated conveyor craft appeared. Six private milita flanked a large clear container which seemed to be the focus of the now wild adulation and hysteria.

'What is it?' Lyrae screeched above the din.

'I don't know. I can't see properly.'

The crowds were throwing flowers, chanting monosyllables while reaching out with whatever extraneous part of their bodies could extend beyond the barrier. The clear container maintained an even pace while the five or so people around me wept, cried and pulled their hairs. A few taller members of the crowd rolled before me. As the container drew within touching distance I bobbed my head to snatch a glimpse of this bizarre procession.

'His majesty! His majesty!' The crowd sang.

Lyrae tugged my sleeve. 'What is it?'

The container drew level.

'It's...it's a...a...piece of jelly...'

The container rolled past, finally disappearing to another sector of the city and we returned our sojourn. When everyone settled back to their business I examined the individuals milling around the streets. Through the swaying bodies I saw a shadowy figure across the street. The figure was faceless, with dark attire, very like the shape in the Savoy doorway and service station canteen. I struggled to gain a clearer view, pushing my way through, but as I reached the edge of the paving it was gone.

Three times I saw the same apparition. I would book an eye examination as soon as we returned to Donovan.

The human inhabitants were the most prominent. Their faces were rigid as plastic, held in earnest poses like the models scanning us from shop windows. They smelled just like the crackling scents filling the packed streets. They too ignored my cheery salutations. Lyrae coughed as a couple swayed past, smothering her nostrils in clouds of chemical attractant. She was obviously repelled.

'The heavier the pocket the emptier the heart,' she called to their disappearing backs.

I politely enquired to an android concierge about the availability of a table in an empty restaurant and were refused on the grounds the establishment was full. The molten rock turned to lava and when I pleaded to use their facilities he raised a square pad to my forehead. He replied I didn't have the necessary I.Q. to grace their hygiene compartments. By the time we crossed the street the volcano burst.

Hurrying through the golden gates of the Palace, a towering shopping centre splattered with gold flakes and encrusted jewels. It shamed any European cathedral for its architectural brilliance, pervading celestial euphoria and empyrean grace. I steamed into the nearest lavatory.

Out of order.

The aerovator was spilling over, so I bounded up the spiraling stairs. Four healthy faced teens were projected on each gothic column singing their latest hit. Crowds congregated around the pillars pawing and craving the holovids. Adverts exploded from the roof, the floor and walls. Each shop flaunted the latest and greatest additions, offering salvation to the empty lives of its customers with the same parallel intent as those on the streets outside.. The blessed scent of perfume shops, infinitely more enlightening than Elyssian incense, scrubbed my soul. If I wasn't on a desperate journey I'd have lingered there until closing. Clothes shops displayed alabaster statues in holy repose, their blessed raiment offering divine succor to those deserving few. Rows of Sondisc shops stood together under the guiding lights of the centre's spotlights. There, two doors down, the sign.

I was within easy reach of the toilet.

The door blew open.

Fortunately the beatific perfume from the upper floor masked the buckets of dung rolling down my legs. Even better luck, our uniforms are sealed in thick boots. I waddled past a fracas outside a Sondisc emporium. Three private militiamen were manhandling a middle aged human woman. I tried to slink by unnoticed but she reached a trembling hand for my badge.

'Sheriff, sheriff, help me please.'

Lyrae was waiting down on the ground floor. My cheeks were red raw and my boots were truly filled. A militiaman dragged her back inside the shop. Not now, not here...

'Yes consumer, how may I assist you?'

The militiaman's free hand stopped short of my squirming intestines. He turned his palm up.

'Nothing to trouble yourself with sheriff, we have this.'

He was a Fronorian, an early simian/sauroped hybrid. He must have caught the sludge bubbling in my trousers because he visibly winced. There is no centralized enforcement agency here. All personal and private protection and security can be recruited from the numerous militia corporations found in every system.

'I'd like to hear the charges.'

There was a brief glimpse of relief on the woman's face. A small crowd gathered around us, some breaking from the sideshow on the pillars. The youngest of the militia stepped between the woman and I.

'She claims Sondisc emptied her bank account. She comes in to complain. Call us. When we charge her for call out, she can't pay...so she must pay.'

I tilted my head past him. 'Madam?'

'It's true,' she sobbed. 'They want my credit, but it's been taken by Sondisc. They conned me. Hidden charges...' She crumpled into a bundle of sobbing pleas.

The first militiaman directed a scaly forefinger between my eyes.

'Sondisc are one of the best, they number one, look at adverts. They rich, they be good people.'

My arm found its way around her shoulder. The three militiamen protested as I led her downstairs.

'Hey, she ours, she our charge.'

I guided her onto the stairway. The militiamen hurried off towards breaking glass, as two rival clothes shop owners attacked each other with their products, throwing hats and shoes before whipping each other with shiny belts and necklaces.

The first militiaman noticed the bare patch where my badge should be.

'Hi, he's no sheriff.'

'We tell the fiscal,' they shouted while they separated the owners rolling around on the floor tangled in their own trousers and shirts.

I left her to slide down to the bottom floor, turned and with my eyes hot and my mouth stiffen and my lips reeled. I jerked a flat thumb to the now baying crowd congregating around the combatants. .

'You do that son.'

I assured the woman justice would prevail. We walked with her to a hovercraft parked close to a steep sided canyon running alongside the Palace. On the distant floor groups of grey ragged skeletons fought over scraps of food in a mushrooming cloud of dust. One of them spotted us, glancing up, pleading merciful eyes shining from the ashen face. Some drank from puddles like dogs while a woman wearing greasy grey hair caught a handful of flies, crushed them then cupped the black mush between her shriveled gums

'Who are they?' I asked the woman as she clambered into the craft. She shook her head.

'I don't know, probably crybabies who can't keep up. Too lazy to work. Resentful of everyone's success I suppose.' The cabin door shut and she waved goodbye as the craft rose steadily above us.

We sat in a nearby park with frozen aldjuice desserts after I paid half my weekly salary to use a public leisure scheme where I cleaned the bottom half of my body. The aldjuice was melting over my fingers as I watched a troupe of children, all matching uniform and headwear being ushered into their school skiff. Lyrae was already licking her sticky fur when I noticed my treat was a purple pool on the hot paving.

'Cheer up, we'll find them. Just need to keep on the hunt.'

I sighed through my nostril as I threw the stick into the spotlessly empty bin. I leaned my back off the bench and sat propping my head up, hands on cheeks.

'It's not that, I...I don't know.'

She curled her arm around my shoulders.

'I'm a dumb shit. No, really I am. I'm not smart, look at everyone back there, they've found it. They're clued up, they've read the memo.'

Lyrae tapped my knee.

'Come on, let's get out of here.'

Those were the most welcome words I'd heard anyone utter in three years.

Chapter 8

We flew rapidly from Jagger 2 pushing the velocity metre to eighty percent, puncturing deep space, cruising without positive destination or navigation marker. We talked for a while regarding our options. I considered this wild goose chase as some sadistic example the Procurator's was setting me.

'We need to find out who has the ability to reset and reprogram a frigate. Then we draw up a suspect list.'

'Whoever wiped the drive probably did the same for the Elyssian. I think we should go to Sagittarius. See if we can interrogate or bribe local crime lords.'

The idea was ludicrous. We'd be sniffed out for the saps we were. However, my stomach warmed to her suggestion even if my head screamed in protest. She played with several interlocking menus on her Sondisc as I inquisitively watched on. It was the standard undergraduate model, could access most domestic frequencies and bands, was routed to the central database and had a smidgen of memory for personal use. The self protection function consisted of dual incapacitation beams one of which is a HI infrasound transmitter and a single ST shot, enough to kill at least one hostile presence. I removed my issued piece, slightly larger, with a silver and gold finish.

'Wait until you get one of these. It has a battery life of five years, a Narcon triple processor and you receive a buyback option with each new model. I can enter any infobank without pre warranted cause and can store two hundred octobytes of personal data. There are four kill ratios with a selection of ion beam, thermodynamic torch, single pulse for distance and repeater shot for multiples. With four mini thorn grenades you're a veritable one man army.'

She was obviously stunned into awed silence when I rotated the device in my palm. I turned to give her a reassuring smile that she would take as much pride in owning one as I did and saw her face was buried in a cross examination of Sagittarian outlaws.

She never showed the slightest interest in or heard a single word I said.

I flew around for a while, unable to gather the slightest droplets of a plan or follow through of our recent let downs and setbacks. For the next hour I took us for a cruise. In our slipstream we left long convoys of freighters, local patrol ships, individual traders and sleek corporation craft. As we took a lonely course we would pass bounty hunters, lone wolf packs and privateers keeping a full solarspheric distance from Jagger 2. The volume of shipping eventually thinned out to solo ships whose purpose was veiled by keeping a long watch on us. Our presence still carried some weight at least among the elementary members of this area. I suppressed the antigravity conditioner by a hair, allowing us to sense the shift and pulse of space travel, the almighty acceleration and thrill of turning and dipping. I played dodge the asteroids, scorched the surface of moons, evened out then performed a complete orbit of a liquid planet. I thoughtlessly flew on impulse and inkling without preset destination. Pooling the power from the other systems I filled the engine with as much energy as it could regulate. We powered with impossible momentum as I spurred our ship to the conformed limits. A few lights turned orange so I acquiesced with the corvette's concern and cooled off.

We left the Jagger system as remote and tiny bodies circling in space. Soon, they left the scope of the radar and we were in an empty ocean of unseen waves. I felt sleepy so I relaxed in my seat, surrendering control to the corvette's A.I drive. We drifted among the delicacy of atomic balance and I closed my eyes.

So where now? We had been given the mother of all bum steers by the very people we needed assistance from. The Syndicate's omniscient presence and monitoring parameters spanning the galaxy should have picked up the frigate within seconds. The whole mission was abnormal. From the Procurator's humiliating cuff off to the uncooperative attitude of the officials concerned. It seemed like a bad dream, or would do if I actually had any experience of them. Perhaps the Syndicate was stumped with this one, perhaps we, Lyrae and I were the only one for this job after all. Sagittarius was the logical hideout. How two humans, fairly below average prisoners by all accounts could be responsible for the theft of a Syndicate battleship was preposterous? This Elyssian was clearly the brains behind the outfit. Yet no records existed: Must be an exceedingly singular talent.

I must have snoozed for a while; I was aroused by a low warning tone from the Corvette's comms. Lyrae was inserting the Sondisc into her belt when I resumed control of the ship.

A slow pulse appeared on the radar screen. I turned to the source, reducing speed while arming weapons. The communication sensors were freaking out, showing colossal magnetic fields. I stopped the corvette and we squared up directly, front on, with the energy source. The radiation shields automatically raised and the cabin began an internal purification cycle. All we saw was space between the happy lights sparkling.

'What is it? A ship on cloak?'

'Too massive a presence.'

I launched our probe, watched it scoot off towards the energy,
Mere seconds passed before it vanished off screen. Now I was
worried. A soft, fleeting thought touched my forehead. I switched
on the cosmic ray enhancer. From the edge of the radar a burning
violet circle flickered. I watched Lyrae contemplating the invisible
menace ahead,

'Could be a neutron star?'

'Soft gamma ray repeater?'

We watched the stars some more. Although we were stationary,
the violet circle was creeping closer.

'I think we ought to change course.'

'Sagittarius?'

'Yeah, come on.'

It was the longest Einstriv countdown I ever suffered, but with a
clunk, a whine and the welcome distortion of everything around us
we blew the hell out of there sharpish.

Chapter 9

I stole a peep at Lyrae and was startled by her green stare.

'Your dad isn't too happy about you being sheriff.'

Two days ago I would have volleyed a muttered excuse. I drew a long puff through my nostrils then pushed out the fumes of my stale breakfast.

'He thinks I've wasted my life. He thinks my sparing visits are to spite him. He doesn't see that without us, every low life in the galaxy would be queuing up to scoop his brains out and use his skull as a piss bowl. Anyway, what about your own parents?'

She sat up, yawned, stretched and picked her claws with her teeth.

'Both my parents are dead.'

'Oh, I'm so sorry.'

She washed her face, soothed her brow, stroked her whiskers and flapped her ears.

'They were murdered in the last year of the Reptoid wars. I was brought up by my uncle Ghee. He encouraged me to be a sheriff,' she added casually.

'Oh.'

'I piloted a gunship into a Reptoid missile dump. Shot down three lizard scouts and an interceptor. It was our final sortie before the ceasefire.'

'Ah.'

'What about you? Why did you join?'

'I wanted to see something more than blue forests and pink seas.' She continued staring across, prompting further extrapolation.

'I don't really belong there. My father's right. Without the hypothalamus configuration...I was always looking for the next big bang, prove my elusive worth. Test myself. Besides I got in with a bad crowd. Needed to save myself.'

She whispered with an unbearable seductiveness, 'have you?'

Four red dots flashed before us followed by the corvette warning us we were being diverted and a return to space time continuum was imminent.

The spiraling tunnel shriveled, revealing the twisting stars and iridescent clouds of gas as we scraped under the hull of a class 4 destroyer ripped apart like tissue. We slowed to avoid tumbling flight decks and chewed dorsal fins. Puffs of flame erupted from glowing fragments, scattered innards and scorched noses littered our view. I checked our navigation update. This immense graveyard was the site of the last Reptoid – Kitt battle. The occasional asteroid rolled past in this jungle of Ferrotone and Hydrothene flotsam. I adjusted the scanner to cover a one hundred thousand kilometre radius. The screen returned only our own smudgy reflections.

Areas like this were a haven for scavengers and down at heel pirates, newly released criminals looking for a scratch back to the big time. Here a desperate renegade could remain mostly undetected.

Lyrae rested her chin on a clenched hand.

'Anything?'

.No, not a blip.'

'Any probes left?' Lyrae asked hopefully.

'No.'

The corvette swooped under a crumpled salamander, the bridge exposed revealing cables and wires growing like tendrils from the burst command panel. The Xin Feng, the ship's primary weapon was suspended, hanging loose by a solitary strut. We swung broadsides, following the scorch marks scoring the length of the flank. Suddenly Lyrae's head whipped forward.

'Did you see that?

We zeroed on the scanner monitor.

Nothing.

I selected fully manual and circled the wreck.

'There!'

A yellow flicker danced on the monitor.

This was the perfect place for an ambush. I swore aloud. Fidgeting in my seat I engaged whisper mode, edging towards the flicker growing stronger, brighter and healthier.

Directing the corvette nearer the source we slipped between indistinguishable lumps, debris and the shell of a Dragon. The blip grew, floating like a beacon drawing us towards its glimmering heart. I increased velocity to breeze, weaving and ducking through the scrap. As we sailed forth I realised whoever it was could also see us. Lyrae held the weapons pad firmly, ready to fry our companion on the slightest indication of attack. I brought our ship to a dead stop.

'What, what is it?'

'Whoever this is…is probably playing the same game as us.' I answered.

A growing tension groaned like tight cables, my stomach puckered and my palms itched: Fear or premonition?

As much as I scoffed and scorned my own people for their hazy ways and refutation of clear logic, I breathed deep, slowed my heart rate to release the anxiety to depart like the stale breath. I guided the ship with intangible instinct and simply guessed our way forward.

Then, directly ahead a glint, a sliver, the flash of a ship's screen, 'There' I panted.

'Yes, I see it. Try to move closer.'

Opting for silent running, we drifted loosely towards who whatever it was.

'It's a Pantera II!' Lyrae yelled in my ear.

The blue and red navigation lights were clearly switched off, the deck lights were killed. The sleek destroyer without a cloaking mechanism was lying in wait for us in dim concealment. The flotsam and jetsam harried us; the chasm of deep space surrounded our standoff with typical apathetic distance.

I nudged the corvette's wedge nose ahead. A red streak flashed above our roof. Lyre stabbed the communication button, slapped up a channel and roared:

'I'm a Kitt, hold fire!'

'What are you doing?'

'Don't worry only a Kitt can pilot our vessels. Genetic recognition filters.'

The holoimager crackled and fizzed.

'Identify yourself.'

Lyrae leaned her black nose into the frying cloud, almost touching the holoplatform.

'Lyrae Tcheetz, Syndicate sheriff.'

The holoplatform buzzed. 'G's girl? You in cloak?'

'Yuss. Permission to board?'

A long minute passed. We sat in silent anticipation.

'Granted.'

I de-cloaked seconds after the Pantera's lights materialised. The battleship was sleek, the nose and body oval layers, ending in a bulbous tail. We docked and were met by a reception of two Kitt guards, their uniforms scorched and torn at the shoulders. The tallest had patches of fur missing between his ears. Both carried the standard plasmat carbines.

'Come with us.'

Chapter 10

We were led through corridors missing panels and loose plates with sections of flooring buckled or replaced by makeshift plates. Lighting cases were cracked or smashed. We trod through the dim tunnel, took an elevator to the upper deck and were guided to the bridge.

A bedraggled crew of Kittens was clustered around, repairing, scanning, issuing instructions, adjusting power bands and logging our arrival.

A stocky Kitten the same height as Lyrae rose from the captain's chair. He approached, extending a formal greeting. The two Kittens rubbed cheeks.

'Sheriff.'

'Captain.'

He was a graying tom with barely a whisker left on his face. His right eye was inflamed and weeping pus. The left was covered with a patch. When he touched my palm I noticed the middle finger was missing.

'Sheriff.' he repeated.

'Captain.'

His grin widened, revealing yellow fangs.

'If only. The name's Ren. Ren Fluex'

He indicated a low table where we could sit. Promptly three glasses of Lactodrene arrived. I hate the stuff but took a sip. Call of duty and all that.

'What are you doing so far from your prefecture and with an Elyssian in tow? Bit out of your territory, no?'

Lyrae eagerly supped her drink while Ran nodded at my end of the table. He looked as if her were falling asleep.

'We are tracking three fugitives.' She placed her glass on the table. 'Two humans and an Elyssian. They killed a batch of Terrarians and hijacked a Syndicate frigate. Sagittarius seemed a reasonable place to start hunting. What are you doing here? Are you a salvage unit?'

Ren licked his lips. He gave himself a moment to settle in his chair. The tip of a claw hung from a finger tip which scratched his neck. Some of his crew left their posts, bleeding from wounds while others replaced them. Ren placed his hands on dirty knee pads and locked his yellow eye on Lyrae.

'We are barely holding on. Part of a fading skirmish line holding the Reptoids back. In fact just before your arrival we discovered our sister ship was...'

His tone sank. A single tear cleansed the weeping pus from his red eye.

I waited until his grief subsided before asking as delicately as I could project.

'But, I don't understand. Surely your war is over? The peace talks?'

Ren coughed, wagging a scarred pad before me. A grinding cackle broke from his throat,

'There will never be peace between us.'

Lyrae interceded. She placed a swift paw on his forearm.

'Ren, we've been listening to the negotiations every day...I was there, at the end.'

Ren swallowed, smoothing his throat with a pad. He released a deep sigh. I felt the air pressure touch my face, catching the nauseating fishy stink.

'War will never end between us my sister no matter what channel you choose to listen to. Every day fresh attacks weaken us. We are the last line of defence for our race.' He paused rubbing each arm to smooth the ruffled fur.

'Look, you'd better move on, continue your mission, we're expecting another attack.'

Lyrae remained motionless, saying nothing, staring hard into her fellow Kitt's eye while stroking his hand.

'I'm staying to help. We've got a corvette and-'

I launched myself to my feet.

'What? Wait, wait, wait. Captain, please excuse us.'

I marshaled Lyrae back into the elevator which yo-yoed between the bridge and engine room.

'What are you playing at? The mission! Remember the mission.'

'Screw the mission. These are my people.'

'Your people, right. Misappropriating Syndicate resources, endangering your career...and me!' I thrust my wiry thumb into her chest as if my declaration needed any further emphasis.

We soared past three Kittens waiting on the medical deck; their faces looked as if a Cananite had stolen their cream.

'You go, take the corvette then. I stay.'

The elevator dropped past the three again who clawed the air.

'To do what exactly? I'm not leaving you here.'

Her eyes considered mine. Cool appraisal. A strong heat from her chest warmed my body. My feet flushed. As we bounced between decks our frigid postures melted, both our shoulders dropped, the tension in my kidneys uncoiled and her slit pupils dilated, the black spilling, covering her irises.

'You mean that?'

I rested my spongy blue fingers on her shoulder.

'Yes.'

The three Kittens on the medical deck resembled three scalded cats when the saw the Elyssian embrace their sister. They spat a screaming cry of despair before tearing back along the corridor, returning to the surgery for a further check up and a second opinion for their poor wounded heads.

Chapter 11

I put the corvette to work, repairing tertiary armour plates and transfusing power to the Pantera's weapons' battery. Their principal twin electron cannon were placed fore and aft with various support guns including IF lasers and a thermoplane turret. The corvette also bluntly informed me she was down to her final seven T-missiles. 'Not exactly match fit,' I muttered to the deadpan console.

I monitored the main cables and pressure sensors: Two in need of urgent replacement, one burnt out completely. Most paramilitary ships are built with universal fixtures and fittings so I pinched a few of our corvette's bits and pieces, transplanting them to the Kitt battleship.

The main wiring paths remained intact although, again, I cannibalized our ship to rewire the sub circuits.

Lyrae tended to the crew. She issued the last of our pistols to internal security and helped Ren distribute provisions among the depleted staff. A full complement of personnel in a Pantera is roughly between one hundred, to eighty. Today she counted twenty five. We met up later in the refreshment quarters.

'Things are a bit haphazard' I stated over a bowl of dry cereal.

She was chomping on a preserved feche clump.

'I'm amazed they've hung on for so long,' she muffled through a mouthful of half chewed food.

'I've had to strip some of the corvette's components,' I mentioned, hopefully spinning a favourable temperature between us. She either didn't hear above the crunching fish bones and chewed fibres or her mind was too deep in other more pressing concerns.

'She'll be fine for combat,' I offered.

Lyrae finished her plate in solemn fastidiousness, gulping the lactodrene in one tip of the glass.

'The bastards.'

I faked an indignant riposte.

'Pardon?'

She folded her arms, resting them on the uniformed chest.

'The lying bastards.'

I was mightily relieved.

'They've spun this gloriously fine web haven't they?'

Whoever 'they' were I sat quietly and waited the extrapolation.

'The curs...growing fat on dead cats.'

Her feline eyes were alert, dangerously bright, narrowing into contemptuous slits.

Her anger burned through me, weakening my solid torso into a drifting powder. I tried the old deep breathing, taught from childhood, picturing the pink sea of tranquility, releasing the disseminating heat wave in my gut. I tried to forge a word of encouragement but mind and body were locked tight.

Eventually she pushed her plate aside and rose.

'You know where your quarters are, yes?'

A reedy reply whispered 'yes.'

'See you then.'

She stalked off, leaving me with a hell of a job to stand up and ask where in Kon I was sleeping in this rickety death trap.

I wandered through empty half lit corridors, testing locked dorms and sealed personal rooms. A handful of guards remained on the bridge and engine room. I returned to a locked canteen. The lights were switched off to save power. I retreated to the medical bay to wearily seek a bad, mattress or empty chair. A familiar purr startled me.

'Looking for a bed?'

She stood in the corridor waving a white type of toga. I ashamedly flashed a grin and shrugged. She beckoned me follow her, taking two elevators and a walkway to the upper quarters. A four bed dorm was unoccupied. Her uniform was stuffed in a disposal box.

'So, this is it then? You're leaving ASS behind.'

'I tried to contact the procurator but the comms are weak. Either jammed or out of range.'

I dipped my head, arched my feet while tracing the yellow roof lights.

'That was me. I took a couple of things from the ship, a diorod or two.'

She padded towards me, her scent hanging heavy in my mouth.

'Luten, about earlier, I'm sorry. I've a lot to thank you for.'

We held eye contact until my gaze returned to the glaring yellow lights. She moved towards her bed.

'So, which one's mine?'

She reached for a stack of pillows and blankets.

I snuggled under the covers minus my boots, staring into the charcoal dark space above me. I waited until Lyrae turned to the wall. A deep elongated purr rippled across the room. Her lean outline curved clear below the blanket. I carefully turned to face her. An unexpected warmth billowed within my stomach, black petals blossoming revealing a golden stamen filling my belly, chest, loins with a heavy delight.

The purring ceased.

I pushed the flower down, closed my eyes and willed myself to sleep with the last dregs of energy. The final thought I heard in my ears said 'you bloody fool, piss boy...'

Chapter 12

Lyrae was gone when I woke. The white blanket was neatly folded and the disposal box containing her uniform was missing, I stepped into the adjacent cleansing unit, stood under the Ducha, waiting for the cherished gush of cleansing fluid and water. I was relishing this.

The Ducha head gurgled mournfully.

I stood waiting until I realised I would have to endure a long day without my morning ablutions.

Half the crew was assembled in the canteen. I scanned the fur and whiskers – Lyrae must be working somewhere. Ordering a double portion of cereal I sat behind a trio of Kittens. Before I could spoon the first mouthful one of them called across.

'Hey, come and join us.'

I nodded thanks and smiled, pulling up a heavy stool. They had finished their crème feche and were discussing the forthcoming attack. A golden female with black spots was talking.

'Well, the reactors are only 60% I doubt I can top it anymore.'

A lean, ginger and white striped fellow playfully tapped my arm. 'Thanks to our friend here we're lucky to have the 60% Seen the job he did rerouting the sub cables?'

'How are the repair droids doing with the aft thermostat?' a sleek black face with amber eyes asked. He circled his glass rim with bristly fingers.

'Droid. Not good. I'm expecting replacement bearings from the Leon.'

After a few more mouthfuls I felt the urge to leave the chat. I assumed the third was an engineer or pseudo technician. He was beefy with huge pads. I'd finish my drink and find Lyrae. I'd leave on good terms by at least sharing a word or two.

'How long have you been here?'

Ginger lowered his Lactodrene, licked his lips. Something was strapped to his chest, hidden beneath the soft fur.

'Far too long mate. Gunner Nij. How you doing? Thanks for the work you did mate. Good stuff.'

We shook hands then he resumed his introduction.

'Been with this ship two years now. Transferred from a Puma squadron. We're all kind of thrown together, patching each other up. Supplies come in always too late. If you want to hang in with us you can have some Dactene with that equine mush.'

We all laughed. The black spots asked if I knew Lyrae well.

'We were only assigned a few days ago. I think we're hitting it off pretty good.'

She scratched her belly, closing her eyes to savour the relief. 'Not many Kittens join the Syndicate.'

I pushed the bowl from the edge of the table.

'Really?'

'Mmm.'

I jerked back, crossed my legs while leaving a palm close to the bowl.

103

'I had no idea the war was still ongoing. They told us you were in peace talks.'

'Peace? With the...ha!' She slammed her glass hard on the table. My bowl trembled. She moved her vision back and forth across the room. They all glowered at me as if I were a Reptoid. I adjusted my badge and uniform, sat slightly upright. The room was very warm. I squelched in my own swamp under the synthetic material.

'We don't have many dealings with Reptoids. They stay well away from our sector.'

They seemed to relax, settling their hind quarters on the stools again. I smoothed the surface of my badge.

'How are things on Elyssia?'

I turned to the ginger. The hollows of my body were turning cool. I was pondering dragging the barrel of Lactodrene to the Ducha and plunging in.

'Good, yes, fairly good, in a good position.'

'Position?'

'Yes, well placed,'

They all matched each other's concerned eyes.

I recalled swaying circles of Elyssians holding hands, dancing around a crystal pyramid. Flexing my fists under the table, I remembered my father's lukewarm voice reminding me of our eternal growth towards Kon.

'Not bad, not bad,' I nodded.

Instantly, all three snapped around.

'Ren, hey!'

I never saw, nor heard him enter.

Hey touched pads with my company, ruffling shoulders or playfully punching arms. He sat opposite me with a hot Lactodrene which he drank not to appease a thirst or comfort his nerves but with sheer, raw enjoyment. When he finished he clasped his strong fingers while he read my every move.

'How are you, Luten?'

He spoke calmly, with real warmth in his words. His lone eye locked on mine a few times, as if he caught sight of prey, but quickly relaxed again, the pupils regularly dilating, The infection had cleared up thanks to the synsolution from the corvette's medical kit.

'In good condition thanks. How are you?'

Ren rubbed his pads together; chewing on a piece of stubborn food nestled between his teeth. I stretched my fingers then squeezed a fist.

'I'm ready.'

Everyone sitting at the table grew deeper into silence. Only the hum of the food dispensers belied our presence. An annoying pulse in my throat urged me to speak.

'This doesn't have to be this way. I can make a call to the Syndicate. I, we can find a resolution.'

He must have dislodged the food, because he chewed slowly on an invisible lump then swallowed.

'An end?'

I lifted my narrow chin.

'We need to consider the attainment goals, the outcomes of this engagement.'

'We are reasonably hungry.'

'But surely your resources, your resilience...'

'Our inner strength is deep, Mr. Luten.' He pronounced my name Lushen after glimpsing it etched on my collar.

I sat up, I felt strangely peaceful; relieved in fact as you do when someone with resolute conviction says something absurd.

'When I was just a flea bitten cub, our planet coordinator, a bloated bag of fur, watched his people starve from misguided management and lapping up the best cream for his own belly. After weeks of protests and strikes our civilization was on the brink of chaos. Talks and talks and talks with constellation officials filled the daily news items. Eventually, it was decided, that an emergency parliament be installed. The new coordinator was a young Reptoid with new plans for restructuring our society and a miracle economic plan, 'bringing order to chaos,' as the old motto goes.

Well, at first, no one in our valley bothered too much. We were happy hunting and breeding and having a loose time of our lives in the bush. We listened to the nightly bulletins from our tree tops how the fiscal growth had returned and how we were encouraged to invest in this and that product and it was our birthright for every Kitt to own their own patch of dirt.

You see, their world is freezing over, we are the nearest starshine. What could we do, leave them to die?

Time passed and I was sturdy teen with a supple back. On a mist filled morning, the valley woke to the crunch of broken trees and mountains of soil being bulldozed aside. Hovering in the hazy sky we could see the vague shapes of Reptoid cruisers while lines of attack troops pointed crackling tridents before us.

We were rounded up, allocated a plain, storage box to live in and ordered to work to pay for our shelter, packaged food, and power supply. The only option was to wander the dust filled landscape and starve where once our forests and meadows lay. Whoever owns the land owns the living: A concept baffling to most Kitts.

All too soon, we turned our noses up at this, this demi-life and refused to play ball, no matter how fluffy or shiny it looked. The Reptoids appointed themselves overlords, supervisors and managers. They spoke of the necessity of lizard eat cat, to get the best out of us we'd have to outrun each other. I was assigned to a hospice for geriatric lizards. In over a hundred and fifty degrees heat I carted them from bed to dining pit. As soon as they slurped their food in one hole it gurgled out the other. Sickly green slime, whose stink wove into the fur, was ingrained in your hands. The pay was pathetic as well. Worst of all were the overseers: Former military officers and medics too incompetent to hold down a ward posting. They couldn't resist the odd pull of whiskers or fur, cleansing their own shit on us Kittens who wiped the stream of repulsive excrement from their filthy elders.

After six hours of shoveling Reptoid khak one night I stopped for a rest. My line manager appeared, a golden scaled bully, not much bigger than myself. He started prodding me with the handle of his trident. He screwed up organising a duty rota and I was the nearest pillory. I sat and took it, took the dull thumps on my back. I was slow to my feet so he used the prongs. Looking back now Luten it seems so foolish I should have taken their vile temper, the snide remarks the passing kicks. It was my shame Luten. My vision blurred and for a moment I thought I was going to pass out, then my sight cleared.

In this eye,' he tapped an opalescent claw on his patch, 'I saw our war, the soul, the dignity of Kitt restored. In this eye,' he switched the point to the pupil dilating thickly, 'I saw us stripped bare, toothless, de-clawed, our fur sold to Ferry 6 for the vanity of a king.

It's these times Luten. When all you've done with your days is let things go. Do I let it pass, bury myself deeper in my pain or do I toughen up?

I exploded in a ball of fury, the years of perdition condensed into a nuclear bomb. My fear of them was completely subsumed and I lashed out with the strength of ten Kittens. I didn't recognise this power, I felt twice my height. I snatched the trident from his flaky hands and buried the spikes below the undulating flesh. The other Kittens, the carers and the kitchen staff fled with me and we returned to what was left of the hills and woods. Word spread; more joined us but were hunted down to the last.

On a freezing midnight I crept into our capital city, a limping emaciated frame of fur and bones. Desperate and hungry I joined an underground resistance group: Using stolen weapons we fought back, sometimes fighting tooth to claw with the Reptoids. After months of bitter fighting, our beautiful city lay in dust while our blood ran in deep canals to the sea. We retook our planet eventually but the Reptoids revenge was relentless, cruel and beyond the twitchiest nightmare we could imagine.

Eventually we freed our system of the lizards by capturing a Syndicate Dreadnaught, upgrading the aerodynamics and weapons it evolved into a Pantera and so began our war and do you know what the Association did Luten?'

He was hugely present, his breath inflating that cask of a chest, the solo eye melting my rigid stare.

'No,' I replied innocently.

'Nothing.'

The howl of a high alert signal interrupted the pooling sweat between my legs.

Orders screamed to attend all our positions from the overhead speaker. Before the order was repeated the Kittens had gone from serene repose to disappearing through the canteen exit. I too left the table, curing the uneaten food and an imbecilic yearning for home. Ren's intimation about the Dreadnaught still trilled in my ears. Would he have the know-how to reset a Syndicate vessel? If we survived this I'd have to formally question him.

Through the flashing red corridors one or two Kittens flashed past. Neither of them was Lyrae. Sprinting across the empty docking hangar, the yellow and blue corvette lifted my spirits. She was on dry running, navigation lights flashed, the engines were humming. She must be inside. As the cockpit doors opened there was no one there except two empty seats and an eager flight panel ready to go.

A bar of red light split the panel in two. The bay doors were still closed.

The operator's booth was empty.

I climbed through the open door and was met by a dead screen. The emergency warning was screeching, the enemy was closing, I was flapping my hands over the controls, pushing and pulling and thumping.

A green light appeared on the bottom left of the panel. I pushed it. The panel surfaced to life.

What now?

There was nothing suggesting or indicating what switch or lever or button you pressed. I tried everything. Lights disappeared, a girder from the roof levered itself down close to the Corvette, the panel switched off. The panel switched on, the internal portals opened and closed, applauding my buffoonery.

And then, cutting through the hoots, the electro-puppetry and pyrotechnics a welcome voice announced I had three seconds to get my backside in the corvette or I'd be sucked unconditionally into space.

As I reversed through the inside doors, waiting on the outer doors to unlock I asked Kon if it wouldn't be too much to ask if Lyrae was kept safe from harm.

I guided the corvette forty five degrees from the Pantera, climbing some thousand metres above. I chose a mangled wreck which I couldn't identify to hide behind. I peered through the mess, screwing my eyes to detect the first move. The radar screen was blank, the scanners reported zero transmissions.

Between the outlying scrapyard, the glint of starlight and scuff marks on the visor I strained my concentration for a hint of fin, wing

110

or tail. I followed a shard drifting close, adjusted my visual range as far as possible then slowly scrolled left to right and back. I was coiled with tension after a few minutes and wondered of the Kitts were misled or spooked by some anomaly in their own detection sections.

Then I saw it: Just a faint movement followed by fleeting glimpses of shadowy lines and snatches of shine. Gradually the nose of a ship pushed through the dark borders of the wreckage.

I checked the radar: Nothing. The ship ground closer, the sleek diamond of a scout vessel. I shuffled the power distribution and after a rapid scramble of waves and pixilation the screen cleared showing an advancing line of bright dots.

The Reptoid assault fleet lined up, ship by ship straight from the void as if squaring up for a nebula race. They emerged between scintillating star shattered stern, sickly green spinal fins slicing the chasm, the nose prong of a Lizard interceptor darting forth, leading the formation. Salamanders speckled in disruptive camouflage, a Viper's missile nozzle reflecting the distant sun: My onscreen radar rapidly filling with red dots.

Chapter 13

In the middle of the line, three class 4 Dragons, equaling the Pantera's firepower. These formidable battleships proved a worthy vessel for privateers and warlords alike. Dense armour coupled with three types of missile, military class lasers and cannon and a crew of two hundred. Only the tardy velocity and turning arcs gave their enemies slim odds. Extending on either side of the Reptoid battleships the chain of Lizards, Vipers and Sidewinders hung like wings from the oblique flanks. I counted twelve altogether. Each Dragon's fangs began to protrude gradually from the hunched nose: The devastating Raptor guns which could melt irresistibly through my craft. I switched the weapon systems from predictive combat to manual: Time for some fun.

I climbed high, the standard, most effective attack strategy in the book. I targeted two Vipers who were closing in on the Pantera. I paused, allowing them to reveal their opening strategy. We were classically outnumbered, but a Syndicate corvette is a lion among hyenas. The empty seat beside me added an extra strand of tension coiling in my arm. I selected the Pantera's frequency and rasped: 'How are you Lyrae?'

From the comms shelf she replied: 'Good as I'll ever be. Watch your tail out there.'

Three spots on the radar homed in on the central circle on the screen. It was on.

I confirmed one Viper, launching a NiXi torpedo. It made a series of spins, dips and twists. When the torpedo hit I followed up with a stream of ion cannon. The red dot turned grey, the shields spent. Another double burst and the craft exploded in a flash of light.

The radar screen showed the cluster diverting into two groups, one heading for the Pantera the other forming a delta formation towards me. From the visor the Reptoid craft homed in. The Salamanders with their broad noses, equipped with four pulse lasers lined me up. A coordinated barrage of at least three ships for a sustained period would finish me off. I needed to put these away fast.

The wingman landed a lateral pulse of chain shot. Rolling and swooping in a tight semi circle I pulled level, holding my thumb on the upper trigger following his arc mercilessly. To my right his partner's Salamander blew in half before he cut my chase. Someone on the Pantera was looking out for me. My prey turned red-orange-white and I had to pull up sharply to clear the ball of fire which threatened to swallow me.

A trio of Salamaders tried to outflank me. I curled downward then whirled in a quick turn, slowed, pulled back and caught the leader directly under the belly. Pushing the fire button until my thumb turned grey, I fried his fuselage. Traces of smoke and sparks scattered from the hull. He broke off in retreat leaving his companions adjusting their flight paths to line me their sights. I chased the nearest between two fragments of a ripped Tiger nose and pounced. Tailing his slipstream I sent two plasma torpedoes directly into his aft vents. He made a sudden dive, plunging first before he would pull up then roll, hoping to lose the gaining orbs. A nifty spin and one of the torpedoes disappeared, fuming off into an empty wasteland.

The second punched deep in the bridge transforming the Salamander into a geyser of death.

His mate caught me on the port wing though. Banking left and performing a hard loop I met him head on. Accelerating towards him I thrust for his nose. He maintained a direct course until we were less than a hundred metres apart. As he climbed I shot his nose clean off with a full ion shot in the pivot rod; he span off, trailing smoke and flames before colliding with the empty shell of a black Pantera.

There was neither time for breath nor a victory yelp. I was surrounded by a gang of circling Reptoid attackers.

I yawed right, then pitched forward, trying to break the stranglehold, A plucky wiper struck, angling in with all guns blazing, I met his challenge, aiming for the framework of the cockpit. The ship creamed in a white blur. Laser, cannon and pulse fire was tearing in from all directions. The corvette took a few hits, titling and quaking as the Reptoids found an easy target. My hands were a blur across the controls, making every burst hit something as I twisted, turned, pushed every molecule of propulsion from the engine and tried a few reckless head on jousts. The turret kept the daring at bay, sending one off with a damaged wing but still they piled in. I had to ease off the fore cannons, they were close to overheating. If they temporarily went offline I'd be like an Academy holotarget.

I shifted the turret to lateral cover as I took a winding evasive course. Lasers were striking with disquieting consistency. Both my shields and cannon temperature met in condition yellow.

Mercifully I escaped the deadly ring and was coasting to a slow stop, rolled, sped up, spun and looped facing the motley crew. My cannons were creeping into the green: Just a few more seconds.

I was hit by direct laser fire. The shield colour bar was dropping into an alarming orange. Do I risk a shot, perhaps taking one out?

Another hit, the corvette asked if I needed assistance.

Aiming the nose and a heavy round of fire into the side of a Viper, I pulled up leaving the hapless pilot in his final confused thoughts. Using the explosion as cover I slowed beyond the contracting blaze and raced through the fires. A Viper and Salamander were chugging beyond the smoke and shower of debris. My cannons were recharged, condition green.

The Salamander absorbed the full might of 5Ti cannon, the engine rupturing as I hit the nose with two focused bursts. He swayed off, trying to regain control as the ship broke up. The Viper took an evasive climb, but the turret ripped a ragged scar along the cooling ducts. As he fled for safety he blew up in a distant fireball.

I checked the scanner update. Three left.

They approached in a standard attack rank, spraying me with a web of lethal laser. I veered left, scooping up a few hits. I released a torpedo which exploded immediately from a counter measure.

Damn, what a waste.

Not quite.

Slowing-stopping, twisting and rolling I performed a half loop before heading back, flying upside down focusing my laser fire in a deadly spewing screech into the first Viper, who was still adjusting to the torpedo shock waves. I added a couple of cannon for luck.

Two to go.

I swooped in a tight curve, ready to engage with the remaining Reptoids. They were trying to outflank me, one sustaining a hail of single fire while the other swooped and spun on my right side, being kept at bay by the turret. Their reflexes were strong though, my hull was sparked while I was evading him while the other had me fixed all the while, mirroring my moves, luring me into a gradual snare while his mate peppered me. I glanced at the control panel: Shields condition yellow.

I brought the corvette to a dead stop. The flanker zapped off already beginning his turning circle to hook me back into the game. The little lizard overshot, flying overhead. I zeroed the crosshairs over the blip sailing into the top right hand corner of the radar screen. Tracing his curling ship through the screen I followed his flight. He had turned a half circle, accelerated towards me and opened fire. I stared, eyes, front, off the screen and made a wild guess where my cannon would hit. As the first parallel burst of laser streamed for me, my thumb hit the button as I pulled up. His lasers scraped the lining of my hull. All I saw was the flash behind me as his Viper was extinguished.

Flying between two unidentifiable wrecks I searched for the last Reptoid. There was no single whisper or twitch. Where was he? Save the odd rock or lump of metal nothing moved. I read the entire score of the radar screen.

I stopped. He was out there, somewhere in the scraps. I nosed forward, steering in soft turns, then stopped, checked for his presence then moved on, threading my way steadily.

I jumped from the seat as the corvette was rocked. From a shredded tear in the side of a cruiser another bout of laser fire seared me. Like a floundering seal I lurched clear of his attack, bumping into the piece of a tail fin. Shields orange.

Shuttling to full speed I made an insane series of moves. Still he clawed me in a ruthless pounding. He was tearing me apart. I'd fallen in his trap.

Condition red.

Another hit and I'd be joining his pals in this forgotten graveyard.

I ranked up full speed taking each hit, each blow. He was directly in my wake. I had one line of shield left, the corvette was howling in repeated warnings and threats as the recharging system was strained to the wire. It was hopeless; he was too quick, too strong. I barked a volcanic mouthful of spittle on the radar screen. That it ends like this? Shafted by an ice brained lizard?

Then, I did something, something every child does when in this situation.

I hit the brakes.

There he was in full pursuit charging into my engines. At least I'd take him with me.

Fortunately a pilot with lesser reactions would have slammed head first into my rear. All I had to do was follow his climb. Without remorse or pity, I gave him my all, spearing his soft underbelly in a flash of light.

As he whirled into a lone rock, a huge crack of light appeared port side. I changed to remote vision and looked appalled on the main battle. The Pantera was besieged on all sides. She looked as if she were about to collapse under a world of fire.

Now the Dragons were coasting in, a frantic exchange of fire volleyed between the Pantera and the Reptoid battle cruisers. The Pantera stabbed a couple of Javelins into the belly of the nearest Dragon, the exhaust trails zipping directly into the hull's weak point – the gap between carapace and plastron. Their countermeasure disintegrated the first missile but the second hit home with a titanic explosion. A diabolical rage spouted from the belly of the beast.

I held back long enough for my shields to recharge then pounced.

The following Dragon focused fire on one of the Pantera's engine sills. I was caught up in a bit of a tangle myself with a couple of Lizards. I shrugged them off, releasing three SP10 darts and a NiXi into the nose. The shield energy must have been concentrated on the bridge because when the blaze cleared it appeared completely unharmed. I whirled around to deal with the other Lizard. The corvette shuddered. Another of my shields was down. I did a double loop, spraying a burst of cannon in the rear end. Usually that kind of intensity would rip it apart. It did, the fighter stuttered off into the distance. Some of the power I donated to the Pantera was surging through her, she was clearing space impeccably. In every direction the void was alive with explosions, streaks of fire and whooshing ships.

Another shield vanished. The second Dragon was concentrating lateral pulse beams directly on my back.

I noticed my turning circle was sluggish. The power meters were dancing up and down as the homeostatic cylinders churned madly to distribute energy. I hoped our donations to the Kittens wouldn't contribute to our demise. A red circle rotated in the main monitor. A central relay cable was malfunctioning.

Two Vipers wove through a cluster of small asteroids. I was preoccupied with my innards I didn't notice the incoming torpedo. I shifted the defence priority to countermeasure the dart fizzing my way. It kept shooting towards me. Damn! The ECM must be inoperable.

I racked the velocity gauge up to the limit, throttling every atom of power from my corvette. While my splenetic escape left the Vipers behind, the dart was reaching closer. I slowed, turned and rolled, dived, spun and nearly passed out with the G forces and kaleidoscopic visions before me. I climbed in a full 360 degree arc. I had one shot at this, one shot or I was going to join the Reptoids filling the void.

I pulled the stick with all my strength as if that was going to make a hell of a difference. Still, this futile act at least gave me a comforting assurance I was doing everything within reason.

Here it comes.

As I completed the turn, the shaft of the missile rose towards my screen. Any second now and I'd be lying in a resurrection chamber back on Elyssia.

Two beams of vehement energy touched the missile and it blew just as I pulled a vertical thrust to avoid getting my hair singed.

Suddenly the corvette shook wildly. I thought I'd cleared the explosion?

The second Dragon growled overhead. Another spurt of cannon seized another shield from the corvette.

Condition red.

The Dragon pursued me back to the main firefight while I dodged and ducked as incoming tore above and below my hot skin. The screen flashed with criss-cross cannon, laser and missiles, streaking the darkness with awesome radiance.

I shot underneath the Pantera who was unloading everything on the third Dragon. I resurfaced above her, stopped abruptly then took a forty five degree angle turn before doubling back. I'd practiced this a thousand times in my dissolute youth in gaming sites when I'd skip the Embassy classes on Lennon 3. The Dragon, following my lead left itself beautifully exposed. I threw the remainder of my missiles with full throated cannon spewing on the middle deck.

A little patch of light appeared followed by an enormous *thoom!*

When I looped around I could see splashes of fire, white lights blowing from the visual panels and thank Kon, an entire starboard panel buckle then slide from the ship. As the Dragon fell multiple explosions ripped through the innards as it went down in a maelstrom.

Six or seven of the escort along with the final Dragon were pouring an avalanche of missiles, cannon and pulse beams on the upper deck of the Pantera. From the remote monitor I heard Ren hissing orders, yewling and growling. I hoped Kon was keeping a careful eye on Lyrae.

Charging towards the melee I targeted two Salamanders. In the aching abyss between 'confirmed' and my thumb exerting pressure on the button a new dot flipped onscreen: A large, blue dot, accelerating towards the Pantera.

The two Salamanders exploded brilliantly.

'Ren, Ren come in, we've another guest joined the party.'

'Ren, do you copy?'

'Ren?'

'Luten!'

Lyrae.

'Ren's dead.'

Kon.

'The new arrival. I've just received preliminary feedback. Luten, it's the hijacked frigate.'

My eyes squinted ahead, searching the impenetrable darkness for a movement, sound or light.'

The roar of the frigate's engines ripped overhead. Four green flashes preceded a flame of exploding energy in one of the Pantera's engines. She slowed to a gradual drift.

'Renegade Blue, I repeat, Renegade Blue!'

Further pandemonium boiled from the intercom. The frigate turned full circle and was fading into the void. I locked on ready to engage pursuit mode as the third Dragon broke up into several pieces through sustained fire from the Pantera. I swatted the last of the Reptoid interceptors with my dorsal shots as I closed in.

'Luten!'

Lyrae screaming.

'Luten, they're in the bridge, the bridge is overrun.'

'Who? What?' I shouted in return.

'The Sken!'

Chapter 14

Tuning the intercam revealed the mid deck scattered with Kittens holding off two Sken behind collapsed roof sections, rubble and dead bodies. They were using their hibeam carbines to good effect; most shots hit their targets. Alas, the beams failed to stop the advancing warrior breed. The Kittens backed further to the ship's aft in a fighting retreat, working in two rows of covering fire while the rear found cover. The carbines blasted and scored the walls, deflected off the Sken's smooth limbs which were protected by laminated bracers. I switched to the hangar. Only the sound of pandemonium was transmitted from the snowy screen.

I watched the disappearing frigate's engine dim from a healthy glow to a weak glimmer. The corvette charged up the engines, diverting power to the thrusters. She heaved forward, skipped a cycle, sputtered. Her power was drained; I'd given the reserves to the Pantera. If I didn't pursue now, we'd lose them.

Screeching, grunts, growls roars filled my cabin.

Silence.

The frigate was escaping. Our mission; so close, too close. So close I could touch the lateral fins. The mission, the fugitives the frigate: My fading career.

Grunts, squeals, cries.

My scanner informed me the frigate's Einstriv was in final countdown.

The corvette strained within reach. 'Target Confirmed' flashed on screen.

The cabin fell silent again.

Lyrae...

As I mentioned before, the night before I left to become a sheriff I had an incendiary row with my father. Well, I was the one doing the shouting while he stood in his turquoise robes, wearing the inane half smile and eyes swollen with pity. He implored me not to join, to stay and contribute to the well being of my people and planet. He suggested I visit the curasols, a ragged tribe of crones who would 'rebalance my consciousness,' and 'align the central light centres.' I'd met a few on my wild travels. Self righteous pseudo intellectuals, with little to offer the economical or political social structure justified their feckless lives with random and poorly interpreted lines from the Book of Kon. 'Let all beings be to whom they belong' and such hokum. For me it wasn't a choice, life never is, whatever chemical ingredients are churning in the soup of your cranium. We are all compelled to the good, bad and indifferent by what we are stamped with.

So when I faced the maniacal Sken, all three metres of him programmed to rip me in two, the arms scything, a blur before my frozen face, I thought, maybe the old man had a point after all.

I cleared the swarms of Salamanders with ease: Anticipating their intent, interpreting each wily maneuver then blowing them apart in a storm of ion cannon. I docked too carelessly, crumpling the port slats and scuffing the hull. The hangar was a implosion of violence.

Three Sken had teleported through transpace, via I assumed a psionic interface. Their rangy bodies allow smoother dematerialisation than other species. Lyrae and six other Kittens were settled in deep combat with two of the bony killers. When my

124

blue face poked out the corvette's side door the third broke off the scuffle, charging straight for my blood.

The second my feet hit the deck I dodged a spit of acid which bubbled the paintwork of the corvette. I ducked under a propelling claw and stepped clear of the countering blade. If I stood toe to toe in another breath I'd be shredded where I stood then stuffed down that screeching gullet. The only hope I had was resorting to Kon-le.

 A compulsory subject for trainee sheriffs is the practice of unarmed combat. The Sondisc has four different modes of anti personnel fire including a laser knife. However, to account for all eventualities in the course of our duties unarmed combat is studied in the senior year. Most trainees (Humans, Surians and Nordics) opt for the more physical approach, learning basic kicks, punches and throws. A good smack on the chin is better than stun selection our humanoid instructor would bellow. We lined up one cold morning in the training hall in Donovan. The queue paired off and snapped, thrust and chopped each other into tender lumps and limps. When sparring with a humanoid I'd always come off worst. I'd instinctively block and duck, never applying great force. I apologized for hours after I positioned a low kick which landed on a Surian's thigh. Surians have strong, solid muscle density wrapped in smooth leathery skin. So I was extremely careful, rarely making full contact.

When they attacked me with deadly verve I'd end up skidding on my backside across the training floor or slammed against the exercise bars on the wall with bone shattering clatter. In the changing rooms I'd inspect a new cut or prod a fresh bruise, my velvet skin ripped open with a toenail or spongy blotched I'd hobble off to the cleansing unit swearing never again, this time I quit.

For our final credit score we were required to specialise in a particular discipline. Where my contemporaries became proficient in bone breaking or death blows I returned to my indigenous self defence system of Kon-le. This is the meat of it.

All ideas, principles, materials, emotions and perceptions exist within a spectrum of Kon – the immanent and transcendent nature of the universe. Every elemental force is held in a relationship with a complementary energy. So the roughest of rocks is smoothed to a silken pebble by the fluency of the river. It's all got to do with harmony or something. I never really paid much attention in foundation collage as you've clearly surmised.

Kon-le is the expression of this applied knowledge of the innate powers within the mundane and sublime worlds. As a martial art, it isn't about winning or defeat, but simply the engagement with an apparently opposing power and allowing the outcome be influenced by experience. Yes, as you guessed, I didn't hang around for supplementary classes.

Let me demonstrate an example. If someone throws you a punch you don't retaliate with the same force, i.e. another punch. Instead you welcome the fist into your space and turn the aggression into a deflection or diversion until the force exhausts itself. By applying throws, spins and locks you gradually wear down the opponent's intent. It takes an immense degree of skill, timing and calm confidence to be effective.

I'd never fought an opponent twice my size though and with a murderous volcanic rage burning inside him, to boot. I was utterly frozen in panic. I had a rattling flashback to our encounter with Rhyddian K'li. I didn't really give a fair account of myself...

Here we go.

The training takes over. Remember the thousand exercises, the drills. Trust the drills. I sucked a barrel of air then hissed out the toxin.

He swung another of those serrated arms. I softened my attitude, allowed the arms to reach peak potential then stepped inside, grabbed the bony wrist which required a stretch of my considerably long fingers and pivoted my hips, divested his fury and miraculously sent him flying across the docking area.

He tumbled over like a rolling stone.

Again he launched for me, a foot the size of my thigh swooping for my head. I simply moved my body slightly to the side, clutched the ankle and helped him on his way headlong into the far wall. There was nothing to it.

I merely allowed him easy passage.

As soon as he landed on his back he was up and running with nauseating speed, swishing those terrifying arms, this time with a razored claw protruding from the middle knuckle. I slipped inside again grabbed the wrist but instead of throwing him twisted the huge hand bending my knees while extending my right leg into a basic stance and locked elbows.

A loud crack split from his shoulder accompanied by a squeal of pain. His legs buckled as he collapsed in installments to the cold floor. Removing my disc I selected neutralize and gave him a burst between his beady eyes.

By the time I reached Lyrae they had already killed one and were closing in on the crony, hunting in pride formation.

'Wait!' I hollered, the cry echoing around the hangar.

Only the Sken turned his face to snarl at the insolent interloper.

'Wait, don't kill it, we need him to talk.'

Too late. Lyrae and the black and white technician I breakfasted with pounced in a pincer move. The Sken's angular head slid to greasy stop beside the toe of my boot.

In the medical room we strapped the Sken I stunned with the strongest bonds and restraining cords, adding 500mls of Tranquinol for insurance.

The crew was gathering what power was left in the ship's reserves, haranguing the droid to repair the main conductors before Reptoid reinforcements arrived.

Lyrae was bent over the Sken who had recovered his senses. One of his pearlescent eyes had opened deep in the sockets and was ricocheting wildly inside the hollows. Thankfully it hadn't managed to reset the shoulder so couldn't exert his full strength. Even so...

'We're wasting our time. He won't talk. Might as well kill it before it escapes.'

I joined Lyrae, trying to lock on to the swiveling eyes.

'Hold on, I've got an idea.'

Chapter 15

I rubbed my hands briskly, breathing deeply, attuning to Kon, slowing my thoughts. His head was held in a brace by now so I rested my fingers on his cool temporal lobe, sinking my mind into his visual memory and language spheres.

He must have concluded what our intentions were because he thrashed, spat and screamed on the two beds we joined together. One of the white straps already had a slight tear so I buried my mind deeper through the strands and fibres.

Father would wholeheartedly disapprove but he wasn't here, was he?

The initial images which billowed past my vision were spiked balls, the crystallization of his survival instincts. I probed beyond barbed walls, toxic swamps and a thorny briar before entering a brutal circuit board, gravitating to the central highway of his core processor; a melting, enraged scream. I got straight to the point.

'Who sent you?'

There followed the usual resistance, threats, curses, pleas then curses. I could vaguely sense that his body stopped writhing; directing his stamina to deal with my probing mental tendrils.

'Never, never, never, never, no, no, no, no, never.'

I waited for the incoming pause, repeating my demand.

This routine proceeded until the face broke down, sobbing.

'Who sent you?'

A childlike voice tinkled beneath the groaning face.

'Kaarelll...'

My blood ran cold. I concentrated hard to stay with the face.

'Who were the ones who brought you?'

'Wyken.'

When the face finished another bout of wailing I asked where they were hiding.

A wavering, broken voice replied 'Zela.'

Shit.

'Grrreat,' Lyrae sighed with a hard breath when I rejoined the medical room.

Green liquid oozed from the Sken's joints, mouth, ears, nose and whatever other mysterious orifice they possessed. With a ferocious spasm his back arched, breaking a vertebrae and one of the chest straps simultaneously. The skeletal frame flopped on the bed with a slap. I had to leave otherwise the odious gasses would have made us retch over the spotlessly clean medical room floor.

Lyrae stepped from the decaying corpse, leaned against one of the walls, legs rooted through the floor and possibly all the way to the engine room.

'I became a sheriff to bring justice to this indifferent Multiverse. Every Kitt is taught fairness as a virtue. The Syndicate donated a Dreadnaught to help our cause.'

The nerves leapt to intercede but my cells held me firm.

'My earliest memory is seeing my dad come home, blackened from labouring in the copper mines. I'd leap into his arms and pester him to play with me. Often he'd fall asleep in the middle of a game and mum and I would carry him to bed. In hindsight mum was exhausted as well. We lived in a grid of grey boxes. The cramped quarters both inside and out stressed us to do terrible things; fighting each other, stealing each others' food, acting like dogs by proving our selves. We bury our waste. Everything returns to where it started. That was the other thing, we had to use Reptoid facilities to wash and relive ourselves. When the systems and pipes broke the streets would be insufferable. Paving cracked, houses buckled. When we complained to the local official we were told "you must pay."

I was woken during the night by my dad. We were being evacuated to safety in the countryside. I lived with my uncle, free from tiny rooms and processed Reptile food which ate my dad's meager ages. These things oppose all our natural instincts Luten. Mum and dad joined the resistance and their Lynx carrier was destroyed by a Proton Bomb.'

She pressed her sharp pupils deep into my soul.

'Proton bombs are exclusive Zelan technology,' she said distractedly. Lyrae shot a contemptuous glance at the table and walked, leaving me alone to clear up the dripping mess.

A darkening question pooled in my head: How could the Kitts hijack a Dreadnaught and clean the memory? If so who was it? I would need to ask Lyrae more about Kitt technology, especially how they could have captured an invincible Syndicate battleship.

Yes you do that Luten, go on; shatter her illusions...

I decided to keep hush for the time being. Let's see where the Sken information took us I thought. Zela. My Kon. A race of perhaps the most technologically advanced beings in the galaxy. They blatantly refused membership of the Association, even threatening war over the non interventionist policy of the Syndicate. Their empire spread from the Sagittarius constellation. They overwhelmed every planet in the vicinity with a super intellect allied with some pretty impressive hardware. The Zelans and Associated Species kept an uneasy watch on each other: Each other's military presence a deterrent to future conflict.

We reassembled Ren's body. He immediately sprang into the Sken boarding party the moment they appeared. He had already downed two and had his fangs halfway through another's windpipe when his back was slashed open. Even as his spirit faded and his body was ripped apart he fought on, clawing and swiping as the Sken pack tore him to shreds, buying the rest of the crew precious time to counter. We counted the dead. There were seven of us left alive.

A Sabre Tooth cruiser arrived with a maintenance ship which began a lengthy series of repair. A fresh squadron of staff arrived as the rest were evacuated onto the Sabre's medical bay. I explained who I was and the captain issued orders to repair the corvette and replenish stocks. One of the missile pods was badly damaged but he would see what engineering could do.

I wandered the Sabre looking for Lyrae but couldn't find her. Her Sondisc was either switched off or malfunctioning. No one said they saw a Kitt matching her description. I suppose she must have left with the other evacuees.

On my way to the accommodation deck the captain and first mate approached me.

'We've got a problem.'

I folded my arms, curling my right forefinger which fitted snugly under my bottom lip. I leaned in.

'We need to return to 'B' fleet soon. It means Ren's body remains on board for at least another twelve days. That's three days over our funeral rites. He died an honourable death, we–'

I showed him my palm.

'I'll take his body back,' I interjected quietly. It delayed my mission slightly but I felt a breezy lightening in me when I said it.

The warm cleansing fluid of the hygiene cubicle made my skin itch. When I washed my hair the smell of battle burped and slurped down the sinkhole. As I toweled myself down I felt a yearning and regretted not saying goodbye before she left. I was the only diner in the canteen. A bog plate of meat stew, herby bread and sat before me. I sipped my sibrew slowly and picked at the beef. It was delicious. I hardly managed a spoonful though and returned to the cabin I shared with three other Kittens. When my head sunk into the soft clean pillow I fell asleep instantly.

The first thing I d on awakening was to contact Lyrae on the Sondisc. No reply. I relayed a message and dressed wearily. Although I had a solid sleep I was very tired. A further investigation into Lyrae's whereabouts led to the same answers. No one had seen her or knew of anyone matching her beige and creamy description. I said my goodbyes and left. If they handed out medals the captain said, I'd be first in the queue.

They did a good job on the corvette. The deep scoring and pock marks were refilled but the fore missile pod was removed, irreparably damaged no doubt. She was even given a polish and screen clean; the dark wedge of her nose glinting under the hangar lights.

I pointed the Sondisc and the pilot door opened.

'You took your time.'

Sitting in my seat, wearing the uniform of a Syndicate sheriff was the most gladdening sight I'd seen in all my six years of duty.

'Well, I've a date, can't be late, the mission can't wait.'

She groaned as I hoisted my freshly washed carcass into the cabin.

'Where to, partner?'

We agreed that if the Sken wasn't lying, then our next course should be the Zela system via Kitt. We ploughed through the smoking scraps and drifting wreckage until we were clear of the battle zone, shooting through Paraspace when our flight path was confirmed, bypassing the Reptoid planets. Our destination would take us to the very boundaries of Syndicate authority.

Chapter 16

We didn't talk much for the duration to Kitt. Ren's sealed body, lying in the cargo hold cast an unusual calm through the ship. Even the regulation systems reported nothing but green bars and spotlights indicating all was well.

Kitt flared orange-red, the huge aura visible many light years distant. We exited Paraspace on the fringes of the system to enjoy the spectacle of a Red Giant. As the only habitable planet in the system, Lyrae's home world was sensibly nominated after the dying star.

On approach I allowed Lyrae to assume docking procedures while I marveled at the view. Kitt had only one continent, as big as Lennon 3's Africa, with similar climate zones: Savannah, jungle and desert. When our clearance was issued we headed for the capital, the great desert city of Amstrad.

There were no walls, no outposts or entrenched defenses. From our height the buildings looked quite plain but grew tall with numerous walkways and escalating homes spiraling in great towers towards the cloudless sky. There were few windows or doors in the dwellings and some roofs were simple stepped peaks while ground based buildings looked functional; offices, public administration centres and storage facilities. Most of the walls were while, some with gold and blue outlines. All the streets flourished with trees, wide grassy lanes and intersecting waterways. As we slowed to landing phase I saw pockmarked walls and some lopsided buildings with glaring chunks torn off the roofs and edges; possibly left in place as a reminder of their war and ensuing liberation.

From the window a crew toiled in the heat, rebuilding a demolished library. At least a dozen other were ripping the foundations of a Reptoid chemical plant.

'They're building a new hospital there,' a grey bearded Kitt nodded.

Three stately elders dressed in plain black robes introduced themselves as high officials. As we entered through the customs area while Ren's body was removed from the corvette we were invited to join the elders for a time. We all walked the wide streets, passing open stalls selling food, clothing and simple gadgets. Those people who ate did so in cafes, crowded bars and restaurants filled with laughter.

Silver tabbies, black and white shorthairs, tortoiseshells, the striped, the spotted and the speckled all grinning and eyes closed came and shook the elders' handpaws.

There was a distinct absence of personal and public aereocraft: Most Kitts walked or climbed or jumped from street, to building to rooftop. The paving was dusty, the sun's heat gently pushing us forward along the tidy, well maintained paths. All presence of the Reptoid was removed: As I passed a wide window I noticed a table arrayed with candles. The light fitting above had been ripped clean from the roof. The streets were winding, irregularly spaced and dipped and rose. Where the Reptoid had attempted to gridline the city, the Kitts had simply built new buildings or planted a bush in the middle of a junction. Where the paving and roads were split, the miasma of sewage, flourishing with full excremental confidence in the mid day warmth kept my breathing shallow and calmly austere.

The central plaza was floored with the mosaic of a large cat, the head resembling an African lioness. A handful of Kitts were replacing broken or lost tiles, perhaps smashed by the Reptoids. As if reading my thoughts one of the striped elders pointed and spoke.

'That's the first principle of effective rule; destroy or warp the values and hopes of a people. That was laid there twenty thousand years ago. No statue or monument, no. She is our foundation, the very essence of our being. Our feet touch her with reverence. She is the portrait of Kitt's spirit. You have been to Africa, on Lennon 3 Mr. Luten?'

My attention reeled from the mosaic to the palm trees fringing the square, to the white arches centering each side. I used the ridge of my hand to shield my eyes from their star's red flare splashed upon the calm sky. How…

'Er, yes, a few times.'

'You made an extensive study of the botany and zoology of the planet?'

'Yes.'

'Then share with us please, the nature of the lion.'

I kind of tripped my way through stuttered bullet points of their hunting and mating habits before concluding my patchwork lecture.

'Well, not for no reason, humans adopted the lion as the symbol of supremacy, power, authority, I sniffed. They sit at the top of the food chain, propagators of a natural hierarchy.

'And what of the lioness, Mr. Luten?'

I shrugged. He nodded as we gathered around the mosaic marveling at the detailed handiwork. The Kittens were carefully reshaping the shattered ears.

Passing across the square I noticed the Kittens would kiss each fragment before inserting the tile back in place. Walking under the arches, we toured some of the districts where the Reptoids presided. Their last spiteful act was an assured slash and burn exercise which the Kittens were eagerly advancing.

Towering office blocks were being shredded, stern factories, pleasure palaces, barracks, prisons; all fell under the claws of the excavators and demolition vehicles. Huge frames, bearing signs, once lit by thousands of electrola globes, toppled with loud cheers. Although the lamps were cold and long neutered I could still see the letters etched in hollow phrases: 'Never Good Enough!' 'Work Harder - For Less!' and other curious reptilian codes.

The streets were widening and there were fewer Kittens filling the buildings. We saw parched hills in the distance and I guessed we were near the outskirts. Lyrae pointed out a silvery disc approaching from the hills so we all stopped for a rest, threw fluids down our necks and watched the craft as it neared. It was an antiquated shuttle used now for Academy training purposes.

The shining disc was making a descent towards us, hovering over a cleared patch of rubble. The ship landed gently, with a droning sound from the obsolete thermonuclear reactor. A panel clunked open and I gaped, astonished at the party who were disembarking: Twelve or fourteen trotting Ovines.

These long faced, curly haired people were the Kitt's nearest neighbours, and at one time their preferred sport and food source. They lived on a planet whose surface was one third ice, one third of tundra and one third of water. They were shy, friendly and timid beings but endured a life of unbearable sub zero conditions. The scant food they found was apportioned to each member without question. They were also the most preyed upon species in the sector.

The oldest elder turned to me and croaked in a high voice: 'Refugees. This war has made us some unlikely allies and taught us some surprising lessons.'

He personally walked over and welcomed them. They were naturally timid at first but relaxed when they saw me standing with the Kitts. A few came over while they waited to be relocated and once or twice I had to snap myself back to attention as I was drowsy listening to their sonorous talk and enchantingly placid faces. Some lambs hid behind their mother's fleeces but soon gamboled out to stare at us. A bone shaking explosion shattered the hot air from the demolition of a Reptoid jail. Some Kittens reacted with startled flinch then stood absolutely stone still. The Ovines fled back inside the shuttle. A couple leaned their pious faces around the door.

I recalled a similar incident when I was young, perhaps my earliest memory. Ah, I was such a tender hearted thing, spooked by the slightest clatter or bang. My father took me to Trafalgar Square one New Year's Eve. I never understood this preposterous pagan rite, where all those present were entranced by inebriated sorcerer's tricks and staged magical transition from one date to the next. While we waited the countdown, I clung to my father's tunic while indestructible legs battered and kneed me. When the first rocket exploded I covered my ears, trying to wriggle up my father's tunic tails. I endured a fifteen minute bombardment from above while besieged by the shock army assault of shadowy legs around. From that New Years' day every shot, explosion and blast was calcifying sediment on my nerves.

We were led into a spacious courtyard fresh with a marbled fountain and scarlet wallflowers. The three elders left us and we sat at a small table and were formally introduced to who I assumed was the top cat of the city.

She was a tall white maned lioness with absurdly long whiskers who rubbed cheeks with Lyrae. She extended a paw before me. I touched the rough pad delicately. She didn't have fingers like Lyrae or Ren and had a hell of a lot more fur as well. She proffered a bowl of dried meat which she and Lyrae chewed with satisfaction. I nibbled a small piece, preferring to drink the glass of water which she herself rose to fill from a porcelain spout. As soon as I touched the glass she landed one of those great paws on my shoulder.

'I believe we owe you a great deal of gratitude Mr. Luten.' Her eyes narrowed then opened; huge, luminous things.

I nodded my thanks. She turned to Lyrae.

'I hear your courage in the skirmish has filled some very influential ears Lyrae.'

She meowed timid thanks. She was sitting straight as a freighter strut, hands folded, ears slightly bent. The elder sat beside her, leaning heavily on the carved wooden chair.

'So many ears that, this morning I was told you are to be offered an advantageous position within our admiralty.' She purred this last word from her sonorous throat.

Lyrae dipped her head which returned smoothly to its position, as if sprung on elasto.

'Thank you, it is a heartfelt honour.'

'Nothing more than you deserve. Report to me in three days time. I'll ease you in. As you have seen, we are occupied with de-occupation.' Above us the roaring star burned as bright as the flowers on the wall, pressing a scalding finger on my scalp. Lyrae and the elder's mouths were half open and they appeared to be panting.

'Meantime, I have a meeting with Ren's family. Please excuse me.' She swept through the oval door leaving us breathing the scent of flowers and listening to the gush of water filling the fountain bowl. Thank Kon Kitts are mercifully succinct otherwise I'd have boiled in my own sweat.

Lyrae rose walking towards the wallflowers, resting her face on the bright petals. I sat by the fountain, washing my hands in the blissfully tepid water. I splashed some on my face, immediately spitting free the remaining drops on my lips. The water was briny, with an aftertaste of rotting weeds. Lyrae was leaning, one hand against the wall with her head angled. Kittens are not inclined to weep, but I swear I heard a short sniff before she wiped her face and returned to where I was sitting,

'Right, ready to go?'

I held the sharp eyes for as long as my wavering consideration could bear.

'Are you sure? i mean, this promotion, your admiralty position.'

She patted me with a heavy pad, straightening her uniform collar.

'Come, we've three fast and loose fish to catch.'

On our return to the Stellaport a barge loaded with freshly hunted vaco was unloading and their bloody kills were being passed around. Each individual creature was handed to a crowd of Kittens. The bodies were carried off, eventually leaving only a few squashed carcasses on the deck.

We stopped in the central plaza where the mosaic lay half complete. The workers must have run to receive their free vaco. Lyrae and I replaced some of the pieces, completing the golden ears of the great goddess before night claimed the last light as Kitt's radiant aura faded behind ragged hills.

We placed the last few pieces of the ear in a loose formation, ready to fit them back when a low rumble made us look up. A Stagg freighter was making the final descent to land outside the city. It was as big as Amstrad itself. Behind it was attached a cargo truck, twice the size of the Stagg. We both stood up.

'Wow. What is it towing?'

I don't know it's too dark to...oh. Hold on...it's a...it's water.'

Lyrae said nothing, returning instead to finish the ear. I remained standing, watching the thrusters slowly place the gigantic cargo trailer in a careful landing. When the trailer was almost lost in the nearby rooftops, I noticed a distinct logo emanate from the rear portion of the cargo ship. McB.

When the Stagg disappeared from sight I hunched beside the lioness. Lyrae was dusting her empty paws. There were still a few missing pieces left to complete the picture.

Chapter 17

The Cooper system lay at the frontier boundary. The primary role of the planet was leisure and trading between constellation merchants and non membership civilisations and galaxies. Lyrae suggested we go undercover.

Eschewing the Syndicate Stellaport we headed for Cooper 3, one of the three habitable planets furthest from its sun. We checked in using our civilian I.D. Lyrae left the corvette with the Portmaster, ordering the ship be given a new coat of Tintura, selecting a neutral grey. From here on in all docking would incur a fee and her badge would be a worthless tin plate.

We spent a frivolous afternoon in the commercial sector, shopping for clothes. I emerged into the lengthening shadows and smouldering horizon in Lincoln green trousers and waistcoat with a brilliant white shirt. Lyrae was sitting on a bench enthroned in broad leaves magnolia flowers wearing a black suit with a dark blue blouse. I gave her my best pose, twisting my brown loafers for closer inspection. She stood up and straightened my collar.

'Nniiice,' she winked lazily.

Our hotel was basic overnight business class, the food was cheap and it was in a quiet area. That was until the riot of children screaming rose from a distant tree line.

'School's out.'

We saw the only other couple staying here when we entered the elevator. I paid for separate rooms which drew a quizzical frown from the Aligenese behind the reception desk. The dining room was subtly lit, the low lights placed high on the walls. When we'd finished the main course and waited for dessert Lyrae rested her slight chin on folded paws.

'What made you change your mind?'

She stretched and yawned, shook her head vigourously then watched the animated artwork on the holoimager.

'About what?'

I wiped my lips with a soft napkin.

'About continuing the mission.'

'I didn't, it was a change of heart.'

I gulped the house special, spilling a few drops of burgundy on the spotless white tablecloth.

Dessert was hurried, a bowl of chilled local fruit. I declined another bottle and we both said sleepy goodnights.

We rose early, deciding to rest up for a day before carrying on. I checked the Corvette's Einstriv charge which was still below 70%. We took a skiff for a tour of the 'Boiling Eye' a kilometre high spout far out to sea. The android climbed in a tight curve around the gush. When we reached the top Lyrae held me tight as we splashed through the overspill.

The skiff propelled us to the Vhor straits where we circumnavigated the Carle, a huge whirlpool where the Vhor and Trinl currents collided. The skiff stopped above the watery vortex where we held tight to the rails. I moved to the bow on my own, leaning apprehensively on the frame. It was a terrifying spectacle. As I watched the churning sea I warily leaned further over the rail. The swirls pooled with enormous, fabulous power forming a yearning pull in heart. The spray was a thousand Elyssian flower fairies calling me home, the turning waters the embrace of my mother's arms. As the unimaginable suction roared and spun, the waters seemed to grow clam as the spiral called to me, urging, pleading to enter the entrancing wheel. I lifted one leg over the railing and the vortex rose higher and higher. I edged my right foot off the deck and bent my left knee ready to join the ecstatic head of oblivion.

A strong hand grabbed my wrist.

'Hey, you fecheing fool. What are you playing at?'

Lyrae's voice snapped me straight back to the skiff.

I looked below my feet at the gurgling maelstrom.

'I...just wanted a closer look.'

She hauled me back.

'Get in here, your making a scene.'

The other tourists applauded Lyrae's timely intervention with laughter and shaking heads.

We followed my inexplicable folly to even my fine senses with a leisurely trip up one of the numerous rivers on the tropical continent. The tree canopy arched over us creating a sheltered tunnel. Scoofish darted in the shallow waters while on the other bank the neck of a shankix appeared from the whistling jungle, checked us out then returned to munch on vine leaves before shrinking back into the foliage.

For a fleeting moment I had the odd urge to hold Lyrae's hand. Every time a startled bird or rodent scuttled into the undergrowth her head would snap in their wake. I turned my head from her, slightly twisting my shoulders. Ridiculous. We are professionals. Colleagues. Besides we are wholly incompatible: Both biologically and behaviourally.

Her training in the Academy required an additional six weeks of resetting her predatory instincts. Kittens have a notoriously capricious nature. No. Stick to your own, Luten.

Back in my room I had a fastidious cleanse then sat on the edge of the bed while I waited for Lyrae in the next room. I was tempted to take a quick nap. I was feeling quite tired. It had been a hectic few days all things considered. Between two slow yawns I reflected on the last week's chase, the fight with the Reptoids made me chuckle. Wait until I tell the lads back at…what lads, who do I call friend? And the thought of facing the Procurator again induced a cold clod in my throat. Maybe I need to quit, leave with the remains of my self esteem before I'm chewed into gristle. Then there's Lyrae…Lyrae, starting out with a fresh hard drive and a fully powered reactor. I wish I'd met her years…no, no, no, stop right there sir. The sound of the door slapped me back to my senses and I left the ruminations behind with the light on.

We walked along the beachfront. Sky high commercials fizzed above, imploring us to buy Zigwax restoration pills and Cantabars, the new ++pulse rifle and the chance to win a Quadrapowered Scorpio III.

The setting sun glowed between palm fronds above the mercurial sea; a few charcoal clouds smudged the blushing sky. The dividing lines on the pavement were already switched on, as were the garish signs suspended above shops, clubs and restaurants. Newly downloaded music was thumping from a bar deep in a narrow alley. I suggested a nightcap and we marched in arm in arm. As we were about to step in a shadowy figure crept into my periphery. It was standing blocking the exit to the alley. I ran for it, slipping on the smooth stones. I was so used to breeze boots, these smooth soles were like prancing on ice. When I reached the main street the figure was gone. I searched hard in both directions. With so many entertainment salons and leisure parlours it could have gone anywhere. I reassured Lyrae I thought I saw someone I recognised an old sheriff and we returned to the bar.

The bar was filled with frontier tourists, fresh from a morning skimming the constellation borders in a converted frigate. I saw one or two of our own itinerary from the skiff trip and nodded a greeting. I ordered the house brew: Cask ale flavoured with manana seeds.

We sat at a small table as far from the loudspeakers as possible.

'This place is cool, must come here on leave sometime.' My skin bristled. Did she mean us?

I tried to avoid too much eye contact. I was still adolescent shy of females, especially another species. The petals began unfolding again so I shunted them back into a hard bud. Thankfully the conversation turned inevitably to work.

'We know their whereabouts, the Zelan system, but we need some kind of cover story or ruse if we get questioned.'

'How about we're on honeymoon.'

She drew a bitter face and poked her pink tongue out a sliver.

'What if we stock up on manana seeds. The Zelans love them, especially as they are paralegal. We can be smugglers or dealers.' She had to shout above the colossal song pounding our ears.

'Yeah, possible.'

She sipped her ale eyeing a quartet of drunken tourists stagger to their feet and dance to an ancient number.

'The thing I don't understand is why would Zelans gang up with two humans and an Elyssian. Smuggling Sken embryos is...well any old fart can do that. Wasn't the captain of the freighter you busted a Giggesthen?

'Yep.' I studied the bubbles rising in my glass. Great, if she knew about my blunder then everyone did.

'So what is the real connection?'

I slopped some ale over my chin. I wasn't a drinker. I loved the taste and first jolly hour of expansive pleasure but I couldn't hold more than a glass. I made exaggerated scratching gestures, holding my chin between thumb and forefinger while I tried to focus.

'Doesn't make sense.' She was already ordering replacements while I struggled with my remaining half. I felt as if invisible hands were cupped under my armpits, prompting me to stand up, grab Lyrae and join the revelers on the floor. Mercifully the song changed to one I despised.

A thick mood cloaked the moment. What a dunderheaded notion. Having an emotional attachment with a Kitt...by Kon she was lovely though. If only I had an erotin pill. I'd lost my ero a long time ago.

'I've got it!'

Dopily I dragged myself from the cavorting dancers.

'You do?'

'You and every other Elyssian have the ability to perceive beyond this world, beyond the electron waves.'

'Whoa.'

'Are you all right? What's so funny? Anyway the Zelans have little use for speech, most of their communication is telepathic. That's why one of your own is used, to broker deals and converse with the Sken. The perfect middle man.'

'Lyre yooz a genus.'

She had nearly finished her second: I hadn't even touched the new one to my lips. A lush orchestra filled the bar, an ebony voice crooned.

'C'mon less danss.'

'Are you jruunk, y rnt you junk, yoonot jinking?'

'Fancy a roll...a dive a loop the loop'

'Nooo...Ill'mmm ffine.'

'I love you, no reeelly.'

'Wher are wee.'

'Juss one more...'

The next thing I remembered was Lyrae half carrying me into the airlift which whisked us to our floor. My door was sadly open.

'Night night.'

I swayed, lolled, leaned on her soft fur, and sprawled into the darkness. I climbed the floor and flopped on the broad bed.

I heard the door close.

Deep in my crumpled head I heard a distant trill. My eyes were encased in hot grit. My stomach was cooking the ocean of jellyfish trying to slither out my mouth.

The door kept ringing.

I was lying on the floor between the bed and bathroom.

Desperate thudding accompanied the trilling door. I crawled to my feet, opening the door to discover Lyrae wild eyed and panting.

'Come on, we've got a problem downstairs.'

I patted the air with my hand then headed to the multisan. I sat under the cold spray and was woken by the glass thumping and shouting:

'Come on!'

When I closed the room door I waved Lyrae ahead while I released a petulant puff of flatulence. I ambled along the corridor hoping the gas would stay by the door.

I was still sealing my shirt front when a large crowd nearly pushed us back inside the aerovator.

'What's all this?' I rasped, blearily spotting several well dressed men and women chattering into their Sandiscs.

Lyrae held the crook of my elbow, leading me through the crowd where a cordon of local peacekeepers kept the mob back.

Lying splayed on the foyer carpet was a dead humanoid body. The eyes were missing, the chest cavity was opened and from where I could see several internal organs were removed. Not a spit of blood was on the carpet or clothes of the victim.

'Who found him?'

'The concierge, he was just finishing night duty when he found the body.

'Who is...he?'

'Fangle Shdun.' The other half of the young couple staying here.

'Kon.'

I breathed slowly to steady the typhoon brewing in my stomach. The air was stifling and I was trying to conjure a response before my knees surrendered.

'I've seen this before. Similar to a case when I was a probationer. We couldn't find the suspect. Not in this universe anyway.'

'What?'

'I traced the biochemical and electromagnetic resonance of the victims to a, a presence, let's say. When I smoked it out the murders stopped. Is the brain and spinal cord also missing?'

'Yeah.'

'Yeah. What did he do, I mean what was his regular employment?'

His rectum was looking directly at me, a solitary pupil holding me in a death-fix. I tried to avert my stare but something was compelling me to remain visually logged in. The hole was widening, growing into a yawning mouth. I was being pulled further, deeper into the dark tunnel, sucked into the mysterious cave running deep into his abdomen. I was there, standing on the threshold, the burnt flesh crusting the entrance. Some unseen force was tearing my strength apart, I was being swallowed whole. The smell of cleaning products and air freshener was a stale, distant impression, the mangled shouts of the crowd and Peacekeeper's advocacy a muffled echo. The light dimmed as I was dragged to the bottomless pit.

Lyrae whirled the holoimage on her Sondisc.

'Test pilot for Intersalve.'

The room was noise and stifling chemicals and a Kitten prodding my arm. I rubbed my face and replied in a perfunctory utterance.

'The company contracted to supply us with cruisers?'

'The same. What'd think?'

'Don't know yet, do the Peacekeepers need to speak to us?'

'No, I've dealt with all that, when you were still spark out.'

'All right. Someone else's problem now. Once we buy these seeds, I reckon we should shoot. This is no random murder. I think it's linked with the mission, most probably at me. How someone could kill an innocent victim though...'

'I was thinking the same. Let's go.'

I walked to the reception where the lady on duty loaded the bill to my Sondisc.

The legs holding me up froze. I had a sense of being suspended in a Perspex cage, distant from the smiling receptionist, detached from the efficient Medicrew hustling the body outside. Everyone's face was vivid: Pockmarks, wrinkles, shining lips all enhanced, their voices drowned in the rushing wind blowing through my skull. Was the sphincter sucking me back?

'876 credits!'

'Sir,' she bowed.

'You should have logged in with your sheriff account,' Lyrae suggested: A day too late.

We found a local foodstuff broker who wangled a deal for 500 t of seeds. While we waited for them to be delivered and loaded on the corvette, Lyrae and I sat in the central plaza sipping sweet tea and eating a small breakfast of spiced pastries.

'These similar murders, what happened?'

I chewed my and swallowed my mouthful, gulping the tea to wash the stinging spices and rehydrate my cringing body.

'The victims were all Syndicate officials. Same thing, except only the spinal cords and brains were extracted.'

'Organ traders?'

'That was our first suspicion. But why councilors? They weren't exactly in peak physical condition, plus their security is among the best in the galaxy. Whatever did this had the skills to elude high end scanning and monitoring kit. But no trace of blood? Weird.'

My Sondisc announced our corvette was loaded. Payment was in process. The invoice flashed on the holoscreen.

3354.

This better be worth it I rued thickly.

Lyrae propelled us into orbit while I coaxed enough saliva to swallow the lumpy snack bar I bought in the executive lounge: 4 credits for two drinks and a bite.

Life as a civ is damn costly. I felt naked sitting without my badge among the business types and tourists and god knows what or how other beings earned their way across the stars. This human across from us, kept glancing over, sly smirk cut across his latex face. His clothes cost more than my salary and he kept giving me the evil eye while raising his brows at Lyrae. I sat there and took it. I had to, what choice was there?

Lyrae yawed left, racking up our speed: Breeze, wind, gale. In ten minutes we reached the border. We sailed between two Syndicate DODO's; drone operated defence outposts. We waited for clearance then sped beyond the frontier. The corvette roared ahead, the great engines pushing us deeper towards our prey. I felt an expanding lightness in my belly. For the first time in weeks I felt good.

Suddenly, the procurator's face appeared on the holoimager, his voice drilled through the cabin.

'5Ti why are your bearings fixed on the forbidden zone? Progress update.'

I cleared my throat.

'We have a positive lead on the fugitives. We are following a calculated surmise.'

'In the forbidden zone?'

'Sir.'

'Luten, that sector is out of our jurisdiction. The cost of your presence is incalculable and why in the Syndicate's name did you interfere in a private dispute on Jagger 2? Return to the nearest Association base and await further instruction.'

Something odd was bubbling in my guts, something strangely pleasant, beyond the frontier. My belly retained that warm expansiveness.

'Sir.'

The holoimager died when my sixth finger deactivated the router.

'Well?'

'Well what?'

She squinted one eye close, that grin pouting from ear to ear,

'Here's your big test.'

Pricks of light burst before my face, specks of stars glided past the visor. Lyrae maintained the high velocity course. To our right the Lydon nebula blossomed, all crimson and green and blue gas and dust. Lyrae inserted a replacement chip in the navigation slot. Within seconds a detailed scheme of the sector appeared on the holoplatform. She fed the coordinates for Zela.

'Ready?'

'Let's go.' I sounded weary, but I was unusually calm. Two weeks ago I'd be sitting in the cubicle rifling up an excuse or kneeling plea to the Procurator.

She selected confirm and the Einstriv began its customary whine. The visor filled with spectral spirals and we were once more hurtling through hyperspace to hostile, unknown territory.

Chapter 18

I passed the duration of the voyage swigging a mineral drink and fitfully dozing off while Lyrae attended to the routine checks, scanning and monitoring the various systems. By the time we reached our first checkpoint I recovered some of my homeostasis.

Emerging from Paraspace's confines, the navigation monitor bleeped. We arrived safely. Cargo intact, hull integrity ninety eight and the life forms were in optimal condition.

Lyrae brought up the local navigation map.

Three red dots surrounded a grey speck. She immediately scanned the ships.

'Three privateers.'

She zoomed the image two hundred times. Weak streaks of light were whipping a small, helpless object.

There we were, out of bounds, beyond jurisdiction, deep in hostile territory, undercover.

'In these circumstances we are advised to maintain procedural neutrality.'

'Screw the procedure,' I said, targeting two of our remaining darts for the smaller interceptors and a T missile into the more formidable corsair.

'Best hit them hard, fast and first.'

The pirates, seemingly oblivious to our presence, continued battering the vulnerable ship. I initiated countdown to launch.

'They won't know what's hit them.'

5

'Until they're vacuumed into infinity,

4

'Hold on.'

3

'That's *not* a ship.'

2

'It's an asteroid!'

1

'They're only ore mining!'

We watched the red square of the missile's exhaust window punch through the void becoming a fading dot behind the visor. One of the interceptors was trying to open communications while taking evasive action – slowing, speeding and rolling for their lives. Lyrae chopped her paw on the dash. The corsair climbed then turned sharply following the trail of our missile in the hope of jamming it. The other ship was fleeing for safety.

The missile was closing in, less than two kilometres. We roared in its wake but were losing it. I released the manual weapon controller, targeting the closing missile firing bursts of chain shot. Six energy bolts whistled off as the missile turned to make the final trajectory before impact.

I switched to pulse. The chances of hitting the damn thing were pitifully slim but a further chain shot would hit the interceptor.

One kilometre to impact.

In my hungover state, eyesight duplicitously hazy I raised my eyeballs sighting the fire red spot in my lower periphery.

'Fire, fire!'

I squashed the fingernail sized button.

Five hundred metres to impact.

Instantaneously a fireball half blinded us. Our corvette took the shockwaves while the missile exploded less than two hundred metres from the interceptor. I nearly fell asleep from relief.

A nasal tone buzzed from the speaker.

'Zntz dn tdz xlkl nz!'

Lyrae switched the auto-translate with delayed response.

'What in hell are you dudes playing at?'

We apologized repeatedly until we drew level. The modified interceptor had a mining laser fitted in place of cannons with resource droids attached in lieu of missile pods. A wide gas scoop jutted from the keel and it bore the markings of many a fearsome scrap. Probably a de commissioned Salamander.

A plated face frowned on screen.

'We thought you were someone else,' I bleated unconvincingly.

The plated face revealed multiple rows of tiny sharp teeth.

'Can't even earn a few credits these days without some bushwhacker nudging in. Whadda ya want?' he asked gruffly.

I raised my hand. 'Sorry, we'll be on our way.'

Plated face rearranged his grimace.

'Say, you're an Elyssian.'

His exclamation was more inquisitive than threatening.

'Yes, I am, yes.'

His left eye tightened.

'Bit off track aint yer?'

I glimpsed Lyrae's hand paused over the weapon controller.

'Yup, just doin' a bit of business s'all.'

The plate face sniggered. 'Must be the zodiac's time o' the month, Seen one o' your kind just three days ago. Say, he was the spittin' image o' you.'

I shifted in the seat, swallowed a mouthful of salty slime and pushed my bottom hard to lean forward. My belly bubbled, groaning as a chill bore through my bones.

'Yeah?'

'Yup, three days ago in the...the what's name o' that station. Yeah, Deadwood. Was with two mean lookin' humans.'

I could barely hold still while I gathered a casual reply as possible as Lyrae gripped my bicep.

'Great, might pop by, swap some skin.'

160

The face burst into a deep guffaw.

'Haw, haw, no dice. When I seen 'em they was on the boarding concourse for their freighter. Was arguin' an cussin'. Course I didn't understand a word, don't need to speak the lingo ter get the gist.'

Lyrae was already arranging flight paths, timing coordinates and destination estimates.

'Well, that's great!' I almost shouted. 'We'd best be goin' partner thanks a million and sorry 'bout the misunderstandin'.'

'Take it easy.'

From now on it would be anything but. With that atom of luck behind you, you know there's a trade off somewhere along the line. We were hot on the trail of the desperados, leaden with manana seeds and not a missile remaining in the housing. Lyrae's last words as she glowered at the auto-translate monitor before we blasted off were: 'We really need to upgrade that grizzled codger.'

I read the Deadwood entry aloud from the database.

'Once a thriving mining colony the economy declined following the great zlint rush of 8031 Current social climate: Volatile. Economic base: Marginal trading, smuggling, reproductive marketing. A haven for pirates, mercenaries and fugitives. Traders and travelers advised to avoid indefinitely.'

'Sounds the perfect location for that ideal weekend break.'

The colony was located between Nana and Dell'on, two gaseous planets furthest from their sun. We evaded the hulks of cannibalized freighters and lumps of indeterminate material, a storm of glittering particles cluttering the orbit.

A few kilometres below a dogfight was in full swing. Twenty odd fighters like a cloud of insects swarming over a rotting corpse: A freshly caught mining barge, no doubt swollen from an excursion to the nearest white dwarf. The network of laser and cannon fire was punctuated with bellowing missile impact. A fleeing craft made a hasty retreat only to be pursued then destroyed by merciless laser engagement from a corvette.

We glanced across at each other. My lips pursed while Lyrae's fur prickled.

We crept closer to the station. The duty cyborg ordered us to wait while a docking bay was furnished. The station was shaped like a classic five pointed star. These structures were popular with colony founders, being easily maintained, functional and armed to the guts. Each pinnacle was fitted with twin Triton howitzers, capable of changing a finely tuned, high velocity intergalactic corvette into a puff of ash in microseconds before you even considered arming a missile. Ships docked inside the vast arms each with a berthing capacity for a hundred medium sized ships. Within the heart of the star were trading halls, accommodation blocks, leisure domes all intermingled with a plethora of bars, eating houses and entertainment suites.

The dogfight was winding down. A few ships were fleeing, visibly shattered. One was heading in our direction.

'3.3.4 has been allocated, third arm, third level, fourth row,' the cyborg bluntly stated.

Breezing above the colossal station we spotted the supplementary guns and laser vents on the roof and undersides. Other ships were streaming to and from the station, not all observing the suggested speeds.

An illuminated gap extended from the arm's edge so we slowed to a whisper, waited for the entry light then slipped inside. Our navigation screens indicated the docking track we should follow. Lyrae changed to autodock, allowing us to settle smoothly and precisely. I clutched her shoulder when she unclipped the safety harness.

'There's something I need to tell you. I've, well, I think I know who this Elyssian is.'

She remained in position, her hands folded on her knees. When I removed my hand she stretched her whiskers back. Her ears straightened and her head rolled to face me.

'I think he's my brother,'

'Your brother? Isn't he dead?'

'My father never found him.'

An oily gloop sunk through me, from throat to anus, a viscous poison which drained me. The ambience clouded over, the visor was a smoky grey, even the display lights diminished. Lyrae toggled the master battery and auxiliary reserves.

'Nah, way off Luten. Look, we need a recharge. Let's move.'

When the green disembarkation light appeared we opened the port exit – walking stiltedly toward Deadwood's checkpoint.

Chapter 19

'Business or pleasure?' the Valgeerian demanded.

'Bit of both,' I grinned, winked and titled my head to Lyrae. We might bump into a Reptiod or ten so we presumed she would be my plaything. He huffily ran a physioscanner over us then pointed one of his horns in the direction of the entry pit.

'On you go, next!'

Lyrae kept her head low in her shoulders. We purposefully strode along the connection shafts, passing Nantaks, Voltorians, Pshtnks and Dirks: Thankfully, no Reptoids. Yet.

A sweaty Voltorian locked eyes with me, holding his sharp stare until he was behind us. Voltorians are notorious slavers. A couple like us would demand a healthy profit in these parts and the outer badlands. Good for us he was heading for departures: Bad were the three Reptoids holding court in the first bar we entered. Lyrae found a booth before I swaggered beside them.

While two of the reptilians boasted, dribbled and drowned the music and noise in dirty laughter the third's cold yellow stare followed me. His dull red head, topped with frontal ridges looked like a child's mask, propped on top of a white cloak. His cronies were bare-chested and flexed their muscles between slurping down Ava liquor (a sickly drink made from ovine brains) of which the bar had an abundant supply on display.

I requested two ales. Lactodrene would be obvious bait for the snake. I ordered in a direct but not impolite manner. I cringed and reminded myself I was playing a role.

The back of my neck itched. The cloaked Reptoid moved closer, the piercing stare fixed on my exposed skin. A touch of his liquor dropped on my sleeve from about of the other's jostling. My legs shivered as my feet felt like they'd been bitten by that scaled jaw. Stuck between an asteroid and meteor, Luten. Out your depth piss boy. Take Lyrae and sod off. Now.

Piss boy.

Leaving the ales untouched I half-turned, considering first the red stain on my shirt, then the golden scaled face of the nearest lizard. The cloak opened the game. You've seen this scenario a thousand times. Any excuse for kick off. Just one chink to prise open: One thread to pull, to justify the urge to flatten the poor feche standing before you under the flooring. I've seen this in every system. Sometimes the gestures differ, the rituals vary, but the intent is universal.

'Something troubling you, brother?'

Kon. He's addressing me as one of them, the nadir of Reptoid humour.

I checked all three smirking faces before replying.

'Nothing that can't be atoned for brother.'

My feet were chewed to pieces while my legs were relying on their rubbery bones for support. The cloak blew a snort from his ducts. I was playing their terminal game. In mocking their register and tone I was facing them down. Big time.

The silence between and around us was tactile, the pregnant calm after a hot day's baking pressure. We were four dudes, perhaps alone on an undiscovered moon. There were no timely referees or

165

watchful security standing by. From the naked aggression pervading the bar, they might even welcome an early spot of blood to slaver over before hoisting my body limp with broken bones into the waste disposal unit.

They held their drinks at waist level, trying to read me sense the weak link, the tearing tissue. I tried to find Lyrae from the corner of my view.

Her seat was empty.

I've got the devil of a scrap on my hands here.

The trickle of strength left in my thighs barely held me up.

I'm dead.

The cloak broke into a jumble of giggles and coughing.

'No fear, brother, no fear.' He raised his claws to the android barkeeper, pointing to the ale rack.

'Send us the reckoning.'

Two more ales landed n the bar. The Reptoids emptied their deep drinking containers, reaching for a fresh round of drink. The golden scaled one licked his lips with a green forked tongue.

'Who gets the good news?'

A display the length of the bar showed the different system times. The station was set to the Ann continent on Zela. I hardly sipped my first drink when the cloak pushed his upturned hand into my chest.

'Wellington.' I slapped my palm on the hard scales.

'Luten.'

'This is Raleigh and Nelson.'

I nodded imperceptibly, the typical machismo exchange of recognition among them.

'What you trading here? Thought an Elyssian like you would be well over the border?'

He had me there the rogue. It wasn't a fight, it as information he wanted. I'd played and lost. Might as well spill the seeds.

'Got 500t of manana seeds. On my way to Zela.'

The cloak massaged his shiny scarlet neck. 'Are you now?'

He left two fingers resting on the juncture of chin and throat. An irredeemable insult: The feche was well and truly hooked.

A wall sized screen brightened. The rodent-like commentator was bursting with glee as he introduced the final match of the season. Us versus them in a shield decider.

'Well, I know a brother can take them off you. Better price than the Zelans will give. He's a human mind, but I trust him.'

I used every fibre in my nerves to stop myself cart wheeling around the bar. A break, a break! From the edge of my view I could see we were roaring into the game, outmaneuvering them, winning every dead ball, using a combination of tactics to nullify their play and push our advantage. We looked unstoppably brilliant, playing the best I'd seen all year.

'You not drinking brother?'

The heavier of the two goldies had his head cocked, the indelible sneer stretching around the back of his head. I cautiously picked up the drink. Oh, missed an open goal there. My Kon, come on, one goal, that's all. They've won all their games with duplicitous tactics, feigning malfunctioning skates then within nanoseconds zooming in to steal undeserved extra time wins. Another chance, we're getting there. Oh, win this and all is well in the Multiverse. End of the first half. The ships returning for a quick patch up and charge.

'Not until red brother here tells us the damage.' I used the plural to salt the talk. I took a long pull of ale as he sunk his lips into his pot licked three times and hissed.

'7000. No more no less.'

If I get out of this caper alive I'll retire straight to the Garfunkel moon. I made a scratching motion with my fingers, glancing across to Lyrae's empty seat. Where the hell was she? I supped another mouth of ale.

'Done.'

We swapped battles and skirmish tales, told some corny jokes and departed on the promise I would meet the cloak that night. All four ale pots were empty. I swayed out the bar, giggling at the leering faces, all fur and scales and spikes evading my magic hands. Through the underwater walk I saw the shadow. When I straightened my legs and lurched for it, the shape vanished like smoke. I hurried back to tell Lyrae.

'You are the stupidest sheriff I've ever met!'

'LLyyrreeee!'

We returned to the ship where I was given an antidote and an ice cold spray. Lyrae had slipped to the toilet while the big time galactico closed the deal. She walked me up and down the length of the full cargo hold.

'We don't have any further leads on these fugitives. We've already outstayed our welcome in this swamp, the Reptoids are on to us and you've just sold our only chance of contact with the Zelans, just because you can't hold your damned ale!'

'Relax, it'll be fine, I'm just pushing for time. Besides, the human...'

'Sounds like they've pushed you: Off the bloody edge.'

'Come on, you think it was easy gabbering with those creeps? Kon, I thought they were going to cave me in.'

'I would have stepped in.'

I threw my gangly arms up, hitting the roof of the hold.

'Yes, and that would have done us the world of good, we'd be sitting comfortably in the pens right now.'

'Better than dealing with a Reptoid.'

We sat quietly in the cabin. Maybe it was a rash move. Maybe the Reptoids were playing infantile games with me but maybe, just maybe I was on to a new lead.

'What time are you meeting them?'

'Eight.' I rubbed my face: I was tired; the antidote was slow to take effect. Lyrae said my speech was more pronounced but my head was throbbing hotly.

'Half an hour. We'd better make a move. You know how touchy Reptoids are about punctuality.'

I didn't but I guessed it wasn't as relaxed as Elyssians. I checked my Sondisc. In my new found friendship with the enemy I'd forgotten the final. I waited impatiently for the match report, reading it as it scrolled down.

"In the final triumphant shot of the game, they showed every atom of courage, skill and determination by destroying the vermin 1-0. The losers wait another year, another year of failure for their vile club and degenerate fans."

'Dammit!'

Lyrae bounced in. 'You all right?'

'No,' I barked huffily, switching off the molten Sondisc.

Our history and heritage, fair play and dignity in defeat and victory have come to this: A team that has given so much and asked for so little. We abide by the rules; conduct our business and sporting prowess with humility and grace, beaten by a crowd of mercenary braggarts, led by a lugubrious narcissist who badmouths the game, cheats, connives and slurs his way to glory. I shook my head in weary resignation. It was enough to sober me up.

The connection shafts were rolling with drunks, hollering and larking: The whiff of each race and species favourite poison infusing the corridor. When I arrived at the bar it was thriving with revelers. A live band played requests. When they finished a number they were congratulated with a shower of cups, booze, pink saliva and snacks, some still wriggling in their bowls. The cloak was leaning against the bar. He sidled up to me, whispered 'twenty three, five minutes' and left.

It only took a few minutes to locate the trading booth.

'23, here we are.' The tell tale quiver in my voice betrayed the façade I was acting out. Lyrae stood a little down the dim corridor, ready to haul my neck out of there.

'I don't like all this.'

I opened my arms.

'Trust me.'

As soon as I pressed the 'Present' button the door eased open. I stepped inside and for the second time in as many days fell to the floor in total darkness.

Chapter 20

I was awakened by a boot in the leg and a distinctly human voice.

'You're a true dumb shit aren't ya?'

Surrounding me were the two humans Algae and Perk with the Elyssian renegade in place of the Reptoids. I was held to a chair by an electroneural magnaband restrainer. We were in the frigate's bridge cruising towards Kon knows where.

The male was as I remembered him from the holoimage, cropped hair and dry dopey eyes. She wore straight blonde hair, carried surplus weight around the hips and stared at everything in mild disbelief then would chuckle revealing a clean, toothy grin.

The Elyssian was slightly taller than the humans, had violet eyes and silver hair tied back. His face was annoying familiar, a face from my youth returned? He strolled over to the chair.

'You've been monitored. Monitored all the way.' He waggled his finger, tutting as he shook his head.

'Never trust a Reptoid brother.'

I readied myself.

'Let's talk, my brother. Let's talk, Wyken.'

The humans laughed as he pulled the mobile captain's before me, settling down as if preparing to watch an anticipated vidshow. He moved his mouth close to my ear. 'We'll use our HF capability so the humans won't hear.'

I frowned, twisting my mouth before saying 'What?'

'You're a wanted man. I'm not who you think I am though.'

That took the breath from me. His voice was inside my head! He raised his delicate eyebrows in expectant invitation. Was this my father's regret? Was this what I'd run from all my life? *I heard his voice as clear as if it were whispered in my ears.*

I didn't have a single thread or iota how to do this. I scrunched my tingling toes to circulate the circulation in my feet and thought of a suitable reply.

'Shouldn't that be my line?'

The humans returned to their posts in the navigation and communication alcoves. The Elyssian sat still, blank faced. Obviously I had a lot of catching up to do.

'Oh, I heard you, loud and clear. It's your own power you fear.'

Well, that wins the jackpot then. How about that?

'How do you think you found us?'

I was too groggy, worried about Lyrae and wrinkled to the soles to play this game.

'I don't know, you tell me.'

'You were led here by the master.'

Lovely. A psychotic into the bargain. He leaned on the floor, drawing a straight line from my toes to his. I squeezed and wriggled my feet harder. The tingling was increasing with some discomfort now.

'You're dying for me to tell aren't you?'

He reclined in the chair, rubbing his palms on the armrests.

'Aren't you, father.'

My feet were now painful blocks of nettle stings and frostbite.

'What?'

I tried to control the shockwaves, the heartbeat hammering the ribs. Then, a strange feeling, a warm bloom, a new sense, a presence of...the totality of memory, morality, all feeling woven into a conscious whole...soul...my soul...

...Which was tumbling helplessly through time and space.

He titled his face: The pale blue skin, the silver hair; my violet eyes. He held up a square the size of my badge and spoke as If counseling a wayward child.

'It's all here. I took a DNA sample while you were under. Now, you can accept the facts, face the truth or you can sit there until your feet fall off.'

I'd actually lost all sensation in my feet. My soul was quivering in the vacuum; my thoughts were as scattered as nebulae dust. He rested his gaze upon me.

Ajanell...mum...my son...my sin.

He had his mother's red hair.

He interpreted my reactions well.

'Look at you. Don't worry, I'm not your nemesis. Remember the tomfoolery with the Giggesthen? The Sken embryos? I'm handing you over personally to the Zelans. That was a costly error father. They paid a ransom for those soldiers. They are righteously pissed off having to postpone the invasion because of your ineptitude. They'll find innumerable uses for your blood once it is drained from you as you watch, drop by drop, cup by cup.'

I heard the last sentence as the voice of the Procurator.

The two humans were absorbed in their tasks, silently marshalling the frigate to Zela. He followed my outlook.

'They are our brokers. When they return to their planet with chromosome transplants and a bit of cut and pasting they will be parcels of death from the master. Through them, the Zelan takeover will be as easy as switching channels. Imagine a consortium of Zelans, Reptoids and humans. Cool efficiency, detached ruthlessness, insecure greed: The perfect alliance.'

Kitt, Lennon, Cooper, Jagger...Elyssia...

He joined his human colleagues on the command deck. My son.

The ricocheting pain in my feet soothed. My skin settled. Why didn't I stay, stay with her? Why not for me the dutiful father, the loyal husband. Would I have been any happier? I kept my head facing the dirty floor, smeared with scratches and stains. Footprints of many sizes shapes, marks of similar colours.

I raised my vision, embraced my son.

'One thing. The war between the Kitten and Reptoids. What's in it for you?'

He smiled pitifully.

'It fills my pouch, what else? Keeps the master fed, strengthens and weakens in equal measure.'

We slowed as a distant pebble expanded to a stone, to a rock, a boulder to a large asteroid. The frigate skimmed the pocked surface then hovered above a shallow crater. A dull disc was wedged in the centre. Six distress lights ran along the edge in an alternating red/green/red sequence. It was a Zelan scout.

An explosion of dust and rock erupted beside the scout craft. From our restricted view all I could see were beams of intense laser fire scoring across the frigate's observation screens.

'It's a corvette!' the man cried desperately.

The frigate titled then curved in a sickening trajectory, retiring fire, relaying a volley of torpedoes while taking subsequent evasive action.

Lyrae.

Chapter 21

She must have followed on cloak from Deadwood, tailing the frigate after the Reptoids shanghaied me. A white blur flashed across the OS.

'The catwoman!' Agate screamed.

The frigate looped then swirled. Everything was a nauseating blur for a moment. When I refocused I heard a growling 'Yes!'

One of the torpedoes made a lucky strike.

We pursued her around the rugged asteroid, through canyons and natural arches, slugging two more torpedoes in her tail. The fight with the Reptoids must have taken a lot of juice from the alternators and main batteries. The corvette's aft cannon blew a couple of shots, shaking the frigate badly. A monitor exploded, the lights dimmed and my arms were free.

The frigate punished our corvette with turret fire, launched a burst of missiles. A tongue of fire spat from the hull, the corvette dipped then dived, landing on the asteroid surface in a plume of smoke and sparks.

I leapt for the man like a tiger, fingers extended to paralyse him with strikes to his neck. Halfway through the jump my eyes watered and I fell with a wincing belly flop on the hard floor of the bridge. He strode towards me as I pulled myself up, adopting a side stance and froze. He held his palm towards me. I was stunned by rippling waves neutralizing my nerves. With an almighty roar I raged forward swinging a wild kick to his face. He stuck a finger above my head and my leg felt as if it hit a solid wall. He wiggled his finger downwards and the last image I remembered was his face bearing the same unemotional smile as my father.

Chapter 22

I slowly resurfaced into the quiet hum of the overhead lamps in a bright room which pulled me further into the physical shell of my body. The lights were excruciatingly bright, even through my heavy eyelids it squeezed my eyes. There was a tinge of bitterness, an unidentified chemical in the air. I opened my lids incrementally only to close them before the blinding lamps. I tried to reposition myself, by sitting upright but was held firmly in place by what seemed to be metal clamps.

My memory returned the events of Yesterday? Last week? The events carouselled around and again. My son, for it was him. I knew. The pregnant girl I abandoned six years ago, just a boy myself. The hunted becoming the hunter. My flesh and blood: A super criminal?

If only I stayed...how things would have been different. I'd have been a better being surely? Would it have been so bad? So what if he wasn't mine, what's the difference? We're all homologous on Elyssia. No, the way it all panned out, it was my doing, my own desperate panic to fill a baleful hole: My own ass. Whatever is coming, I deserve it.

That last self pitying thought tore me awake. I opened the lids again, slowly, slowly. It took a few moments to acclimatise. Gradually the shapes and shades of the room appeared. To my left a row of scientific instruments stacked like rifles. Above a trolley of screens, mini generators and power packs attached to multisans, the kind medical practitioners use for general hygiene, washing patients, cleansing cuts and wounds. The metallic door before me had a strip of red lights above the door frame indicating a locked room. When I faced right my heart seized.

Keeping me company in this sterile chamber was a pile of cadavers. Some had neat holes drilled through the chest and abdomen with burnt edges fringing the openings. Some had toes and fingers missing; jaw bones were removed and cauterized. I swiveled my head and shoulders and saw three with their legs wide open, the rectums bored out, clean as a pipe.

Stacked on a sliding tray was a heap of purple hearts.

Purple hearts, the colour of Elyssian hearts, unless there was another race with the same tissue tone.

Creeping fingers stroked my spine. Hair and genitals were removed precisely: Causing them to appear as if they were born deficient of those organs. The area around the anus was also burnt suggesting the method of extraction involved an intense heat. A laser scalpel or VLN light pen came to mind.

The hiss of the sliding door drew my attention from the unfortunates beside me. I thought I was still dreaming or that I was drowning in the side effects of the alcohol antidote, indulging in some wild hallucination or a unacknowledged flashback, some leering apparition called forth from my conscience.

When the first Zelan lowered his oval, translucent face with that slit mouth and those obsidian eyes observed me I knew I was hopelessly awake.

Four of the spindly grey creatures waddled beside me. A sulphurous forefinger   pointed to my forehead, inducing a thin nausea through me, then a growing pressure between my temples. My joints were jagged and uncomfortably stiff so when I saw my arms rise, palm upwards a quickening panic jolted me. My hands were warming and a magnetic touch expanded before me, The adversaries each wriggled their fingers, their ill intent rebounding back from my tips to their own. I tried to clench a fist, cutting the space between us. I surrendered eventually, flopping back on the platform like a wet cloth.

One of them crept closer until I saw the huge pores, the putrid mushroom skin and my sweating face reflected in his black eyes. My heartbeat shot past 150 BPM while I struggled to free my aching limbs from the bonds. He was joined by his colleagues who poked and prodded with platinum rods and needle like probes.

I scoured the walls behind the ghastly mob my apprehension zeroing on the logo of the multisan cabinet.

McB.

Where had I seen that insignia before...

When my view returned to the Zelans I realised I was stark naked.

For a while they scraped and prodded some more, twisted, pinched and poked. I tried to calm my throbbing mind, ease the scorching gut while the metallic hydrutile was on tireless buzzing overtime. Their tendril fingers passed small capsules and plates to each other. My chest was swabbed from an implement dangling from the mobile multisan, as if he were signing his name to a Bill of Sale.

Then he opened my legs. A warm gush splashed my anus.

Oh, no.

No, no, no, no, no.

No fucking way.

I thrashed, I roared, I seethed, I cursed and spat direst imprecations on them and their relatives. I tried to kick and gnash their hands, wriggled, squirmed and thrashed again. Another Zelan held a forked tool against my temple. I begged and pleaded and sobbed as I deflated back to the table's smooth surface.

When I heard the staccato buzz of the surgical laser an agonising pain stabbed my gut. I jerked hard upright, screeching as a high pitched fart tooted from my bum. The Zelans stepped back, visibly alarmed.

I was possessed by some demonic power as the brightness faded and I felt completely numb.

The gravitational collapse of fear and loss of control, all sense of injustice regarding this impending horror pulled a solidifying block of primordial rage into my belly. All gases burned in a glorious inferno of thermonuclear fusion. The white dwarf spewed and irresistible discharge of power coursing through my limbs.

The voice that ripped from my throat certainly wasn't mine; a guttural bellow from the bowels of a confounded circle of hell. My flat teeth warped into thick fangs, my skin sizzled aquamarine, from my solar plexus entire nebula exploded across the room as lightning burst from my torso and I bolted upright, snapping the restraints securing me.

The Zelan had returned, crouched between my legs the laser slowly sailing between the gap of my knees, holding that same cool appraisal, that emotionless face, impartial of detached, enquiry.

I saw his eyes, in my own, mirrored there, getting madder; getting even.

My son, my son, what have I done? All those strident years, the Academy, deployed across the diameter of the galaxy, my salary waiting for me in a lonely account, my son...you asshole, you piss boy...the morbid idiocy of youth...

I went like, total supernova.

He dropped the scalpel which melted through the table and was blackening the tiled floor. His associate advanced with the forked implement on emaciated, knobbly legs. I glared into his eyes with an intensity to match the laser which was halfway through the scorched tiles already.

 He was lifted off his feet, collided into the cadavers, wrestling with the corpses as they tumbled upon him. The first Zelan recovered is senses, had pulled the laser from the floor and led the charge. I sucked a generous lungful, drawing eventually to full capacity and with a strength beyond madness broke free of the clamps, the last strap pinging free, striking the gleaming wall with a hollow click.

Before my eyes the red beam of laser blurred across my face. I threw myself loose from the bed, grabbed his feeble wrist (not much thicker than mine actually) holding the laser and twisted.

The bone snapped, puncturing the skin which tore up the forearm like a zip. Before I gagged on the stink the searing pain in my cheek made me howl in agony. The little bastard swopped hands and slashed me with the scalped.

Acting in a blind fury I grabbed the laser's handle from him, slicing him open from throat to belly. All manner of wormy innards and slug like tubes spilled from the fragile bones and skimpy flesh.

Inserting the laser through his forehead for good measure I stomped towards the remaining pair while the other was heaving off cadavers with stalk like arms.

Before I lifted my heel to squash his face I glowered into those soulless inky eyes. The slotted mouth tapered chin and cold skin were as fixed as they had been when they first entered the room. Moments before my foot burst through his broad forehead he closed those viscous eyes.

Something hard and sharp was picking my left shoulder. The third Zelan was digging a hole in my flesh as his mate swung an electric prod into my side. Lifting my foot I thrust hard on that bulbous knee which cracked sickeningly. He pitched forward, timing his fall perfectly with my rising knee which sunk deep beneath the nasal cavity. When I withdrew my knee it was caked in Zelan brain.

The final opponent was backing for the door, jabbing the prod; losing the shrinking distance between us. His forehead was wrinkled, those insect like eyes were thin cracks. He was uncertain of this maniac strolling towards him.

He retracted the prod, ready to swing. I launched myself into his space, clamping his skinny arms at the elbows while my head butt closed his eyes tight. I released my grip and he faded, his body limply rolling on the floor.

Black blood pooled around my bare feet. I was trembling, my hands quivered and my legs so weak I had to lean on the bed. I heard my breathing, felt the cold air whistle between my teeth. When I found the strength to stand steadily, nude in the room of death I was a Red Giant. Truly I had stepped into a new world.

Chapter 23

The door slipped open when I stepped on the sensor. I eased my head around the frame. Clear. Stalking the curved corridor, ready to blow the first puckered face into Paraspace, I paused, straining my ears for any sound or approaching presence. There were no more doors on either wall. Ahead was a square of light stretched on the floor indicating some kind of open door way. I placed my feet with considered steps and no clue as to my next move to the light.

I inched as close as possible to the frame, concentrating hard to pick up anything from the silence.

'Luten, do join us.'

My shock quickly descended into fading hope as I spotted my elongated shadow cross the square lemon light.

'Please.'

Do I run? Where? Escape? How?

Covering my genitals with my hands I stepped into the source of the enlightened voice.

Steeping through the door elicited a wolf whistle from the humans. I surmised this was the Bridge of the Zelan ship. One of them, the skipper I supposed stood between my son and Lyrae who sat on an oblong box. The walls were framed with windows the same shape and colour of their eyes. A command panel was gleefully relaying messages, blinking lights and frequent navigation graphs and power bars. The centre of the bridge was occupied with a low dome from which a set of lit bulbs pulsed, orange, blue and white.

'Come, come closer father, don't be shy.'

The Zelan apprehended me with those static eyes. From the layer of moisture I read his thought.

'You will pay.'

My son sniggered at my spread hands.

'Bet you wish you covered that up ten years ago.'

I searched his features, remembering his mother's semblance, the nervous eyes, the duplicitous smile. There, he has my tiny ears. Well, every Elyssian does. The blonde woman was platying with a Sondisc, turned to the ships, instruments, checked the autodrive then returned to the portable media console.

I coughed up a salty blob and swallowed.

'Where are we going?'

My burned cheek was soothing although it glowed with an acidic sting. I willed my hand to remain where it was, even though the wound screamed for a soothing palm. The male human scanned me, head to toe. We were more or less the same height. He cropped hair, was broad shouldered and his bare arms hung loose, more fatty than muscled. He addressed me, talking to my chest.

'We're handin' you over personally to the Zelan Chancellor.'

He raised his face to mine.

'I'm gonna enjoy watching him bore out your asshole,' he drawled in a deep Californian baritone.'

I then dropped to floor, struggling for foul and filthy air. I saw the uppercut coming, but with my hands protecting the old creative streak I was caught in a neural crossroads. While I squatted on the

186

floor waiting for my lings to recover I caught Lyrae's dilated pupils. Here I was bare -assed, waltzing in without plan or preparation. I left her anguished stare, turning to the logo on the Zelan's flight panel. There it was again. McB.

Macbeth: The procurator's pal?

I studied my son for a solitary fibre of mercy, a filament of empathy. He squatted beside me with acute, frozen irises. He rested the muzzle of a carbine on my wounded shoulder and snuffled.

'I guess it's a bit too late to say sorry?'

He lifted the carbine, jamming it under my chin, snarling, 'mum died of an overdose.' He pushed the aperture deep, squashing my windpipe.

'She died alone in a refuge block on Hendrix 9. I was left in the hands of a Reptoid, a mean bastard by your standards, but he taught me how to hate. I swore if I ever found you...'

He spat in my eyes; I didn't mind. I deserved it. Five years living in a sheriff's uniform and here I was facing my nemesis without belt or bootstrap.

'I'm sorry,' I wheezed.'

'What was that?'

'I'm sorry, I'm truly sorry,' I said weakly.

I coughed; a pathetic half-hearted thing.

'Please, please for...' I retched.

'Yes? Can I actually presume what you were about to dare say? No you don't, that's the easy way out. You won't hide in that miserable cave.'

I shook my head. 'I don't blame you. I ask only one thing, please do as you will, but please. I beg you my ssrrrgggh.'

He released the barrel from my throat.

'Go on.'

I gurgled, a spiky sob. 'Please, let Lyrae go.' I tried to squirt whatever drop of kindness remained in my shriveled Kon-la.'

He stretched to watch Lyrae inspecting this miserable scene.

'Very well,' he sighed, 'I release you.'

The muzzle swung 180 degrees, firing a shot of UZ pulse. Lyrae caterwauled, was thrown from the box and landed beside the woman with a thump.

The next to fall was my son.

As the edge of my hand chopped his shoulder blade faster than the speed of a comet my son slumped hopelessly. I reached for the rifle but it slid out of reach as the ship lurched violently. The Zelan hobbled to the door so lunged for his legs but was bowled over by the male who squeezed his arms around my waist. Blood from my shoulder had streaked down my arms and was smeared over his dense face. Due to the slenderness of my midriff he squeezed tighter, misjudging my pliable torso. Thanks to my blood and the enforced twenty four hour diet I managed to wriggle free of his embrace, reaching with tightening fingers for his throat. My knowledge of human anatomy is sparse but I recalled enough basic interspecies lessons from the Academy to place two tips on either side of his neck. I squeezed the artery while he tried to claw and writhe himself to an advantageous position.

He reached for my wrist with chubby, rough hands. With his human strength he could easily remove my arm from its socket then crush me. Just as he closed his grip on my delicate wrist his eyes glazed and his head nodded, allowing me to shake him off, help Lyrae and assess our situation.

The woman was pointing the carbine between my eyes.

Situation update.

This was it: Killed by a crooked human on a Zelan scout ship careering on a death slide with my renegade son and a Kitt I fell in love with. Nothing in my wildest imaginings would have topped this for an ending.

Except, the ship inexplicably, suddenly, titled in the opposite direction.

The blonde was howling in pain, her lower left white trouser leg was darkening with rich blood oozing from Lyrae's fangs sunk deep into her calf.

I landed on her back with a running jump across the bridge. Applying a rear naked choke, she soon followed her partner, flopping on the deck then joining him in sweet repose in the Sueno nebula.

'Lyrae?'

I knelt beside her, lifting her bloodied chin.

'I'm fine. Lucky for me, he's not like you-a piss poor shot: Only grazed my shoulder.'

I gently helped her stand on those wide feet. A groan near the door spurned our brief respite. My son was raising himself awkwardly to his feet, eyes bland and bloodshot, his skin a greying hue. He fiddled with his wristband. He pointed a jabbing finger.

'He's coming for you.'

Those were the last words I heard him speak before he disappeared before our astonished eyes.

Chapter 24

I pulled Perk's trousers free and slipped them up my waist, pulling the ezeband to adjust to my waistline. They were at least six sizes too big. I folded the hems up and snapped a loose wire from the command panel to secure the waistband further. Using the remaining wire we bound the human's ankles and wrists, dragged them to the puddle of entrails in the laboratory and returned to deal with the Zelan. When we entered the Bridge he was gone.

I forlornly looked both ways along the corridor as if he would be conveniently waiting for us to politely request he follow us to the Syndicate holding pens.

'Forget him. We need to turn this ship around.'

Lyrae poked and prodded every ostensible control. She slipped her hand across glowing panels before slapping the defiant lightshow, cursing in archaic Kitt.

Two white lights flashed strobe-like above the central visor.

'Something's about to jettison.'

The lights changed to yellow, then red. We heard a wrenching blast before a glowing coal shot before us.

'Escape pod,' Lyrae stated blandly.

I leaned wearily against the panel, exhausted. My arms were locked on the edge, my legs were waning and my poor back ached for a soft bed.

'We need to get out of here. Can't, isn't there some way to control this heap?'

She pushed every tab twice, swore innumerous times and battered the fascia until a forked crack split the screen.

The ship gradually came to a complete stop. She tapped and cajoled while I sat on her oblong box using the woman's sleeve as sling until, with thunderous finally Lyre joined me, sitting with a hand cupping her jaw.

'I don't believe this.'

'What?'

'We're stuck.'

'The engine's drained of core power-even the auxiliary batteries are flat.'

As if to confirm this classified status report the Bridge lighting dimmed.

'Something is sucking the power from this bird.'

She ran three ultra scans with the remaining energy, rebooted the drives, reset the IR chips then stepped back and kicked ventilation grille. I used the other sleeve from the human's blouse to patch her shoulder.

'It'll wait,' she snapped irritably.

'Maybe we can use an escape pod?' I offered.

'Not unless you want to pay your respects to the Zelan Chancellor personally.'

I prompted her to keep trying rubbing my weary eyes.

Without warning the central dome began to emit a melancholic drone. Every light bulb and bar was winking excitedly as the humming grew louder. When the noise reached an even pitch the Bridge lights returned, the command panel lit up and the ship stared to accelerate.

'Hey, fantastic, well done,' I cheered.

Lyrae's mouth was slightly open, her face a blank plate of confusion.

'I don't understand. I didn't do anything.' She shrugged, I tapped my bare feet and the ship gathered terrific speed, the distant stars streaking past the fore visor. Lyrae stood before the navigation panel.

'All power readings indicate 0.3 energy levels: There simply isn't enough power to propel this craft!'

The dome's pitch rose. 'It must be generating from here.' I walked the circumference checking for any blatant evidence to confirm my theory.

'Luten?'

'Yeah?'

'I hate to spoil our premature celebrations but...'

'Mm Hm?' I was smoothing my hand over a ridge dividing the housing panels. The surface was quite warm.

'We're heading straight for Zela. ETA ten minutes.'

She looked over her shoulder as I turned away; trying to staunch my stomach heaving up whatever bile was left down there.

'There has to be some way of shutting this thing off or turning this lump of khak back.'

We wasted a whole minute buggering around with the command panel to no success. The navigation screen showed a grey dot, us, crawling towards the large blue spot locked in centre screen.

The dome reached a triumphant whine as the lights twinkled like the billion stars around us. I marched over to the dome, dug my fingers between the panels and pulled. Lyrae joined me and inserting her claws tore the panel with a virile grunt.

She dropped the panel and we both gawped at the impossible, the improbable, the preposterous, the unlikely but outstandingly plain fact we were travelling in a biomechatronic wonder.

Suspended in a shallow tank of clear fluid, with an array of fanged wires and nodes attached to the grey surface were four brains of equal size with attached to spinal cords disappearing into each side, each distinctly alive, distinctly human. Lyrae translated the three digital symbols flashing on the chamber wall.

'37 degrees.'

She rapidly checked the entire interior.

'From the looks of it, this is a prototype. A self propelled craft. No need for a crew. If the Reptoids get hold of this...'

I rested my hand on her arm.

'My Kon, the renegades. My, my son, they're all caught up in this...these mercenaries.'

A green and orange light sequence beeped and flashed from the command panel.

'We're entering Zelan space.'

Lyrae ran to the carbine, lying tucked neatly into the skirting of the wall. She checked the power level, raised the butt to her cheek and took aim into the dome.

'Whoa, whoa, what are you doing?' I made a grab for the barrel.

'We have to, there's no other way. Do you want to lie and watch your rectum spooned out like a worm in a piece of fruit? Besides, this'll set them back a few years. Stand aside.'

'It's murder!'

'Those things aren't people. Without a body these are comatose appendages Four semi lives or four million real ones, now back off.'

 As I swiped the barrel from her grip a blinding flash knocked me ground wards. A painful jab stabbed the sides of my feet, a hot tear sliced my belly, my fingers swelled; my skull was being crushed in the jaws of a Narlach as I slammed hard on the deck.

'Luten? *Luten?*'

 My eyes opened involuntarily. Her voice and face faded into a golden summer haze, asking the old questions...I blew a slow breath, breathing an airy space, blowing the old choking dust free, melting the glacier crushing my skull, redistributing oxygen to the cortisol jam.

Then it started.

Chapter 25

As the pain dissolved; the hot scar across my cheek, my seeping shoulder, the ache in my legs, the excruciating electromagnetic field of my home word, the countless losses, my son...it's all being taken, the imprint of my badge, the stiff uniform, the hunger...free from the material push and pull, this unfolding, enfolding, folding universe...

Charge carriers, electrons, ions, the subatomic particle mess that was my body became a current of rain played backwards.

All this boiling frustration; borne of an unmanned craft, diminishing in space.

'Luten, can you hear me? The Zelans, they'll be on to us in minutes!'

The Zelans, minutes...hee hee...it doesn't matter Lyrae, none of it matters...I'm dead now. Is this it? After all that fuss and fear, hoarding the credits, saving for my dream castle on Jagger, the tears and gut wrenching clawing for safety in a job I wasn't much good at? Well...

I followed the last breath through the roof of the craft. There was Lyrae shaking my useless body, the four brains still frying with electrical impulses in the chamber. Farewell my corpse, adios you seditious bacteria, you mutinous disease, goodbye treacherous tumours, we part at last weak traitor.

Leaving the outer radiation shield of the ship I rode a geomagnetic storm, surfing a river of protons. I had no cells, I was free of poison. Downriver I flowed, filled with joyful abandon and infantile glee. As I rolled forward I caught sight of my wake.

The Zelan ship veered wildly off course as if smacked by a Kon sized bat, directly into the vicinity of the galaxy's centre.

I fretted tightly; Lyrae is probably too concerned for my life to notice. I need to get back. I flapped hysterically but remained adrift. No, I wasn't drifting, I was drowning...

The great celestial sea of Sagittarius engulfed me. The particles, forming a loose hand oscillated, silver and gold glitter dancing the light fantastic. In fact espying the space where my chest was, the familiar curve was replaced by an electroluminescence, a radiant web of luminous efficacy. I saw though clear shallows of delight, wallowing in gloomy depths, slipped across arctic frigidity, I surfaced through breezes and winds and electrical storms until in rational calm I saw the Zelan craft. It had deviated off course and was roaring, inexorably into the direction of that swirling, supermassive black hole...

In the squalid rush and fearful chaos of my fretful mind I lost all sense, in desperate and primitive dismay I cried for help.

Expecting some galactic ray to beam in and teleport us to safety, I waited for the miracle. When it became disquietingly transparent my cries were unheeded I melted into despair. This was all so unnecessary, so pointless, such a futile end to two worthwhile lives. Well, one at least.

It was then I noticed I wasn't breathing. Therefore, how could I drown?

An ecstatic calm, a subatomic, ionizing peace glowed within my presence. Take it easy, let it pass...

I'll never get out of this world alive.

Thanks Hank.

I pulled a few strokes, a front crawl forward through the wavelengths. In place of my hands was a pulsing long wave ripple.

Knowing nothing other than just getting my head down and willing myself forward I soon caught the Zelan craft, spying it through a cloud of dust and gas. I had no idea what I was doing and mused whether this wasn't some hallucination brought on by my blackout. Spectral fumes flared around, the ship was glowing and I guessed we were way past worrying about being caught by pursuing Zelans.

My hands shifted orange then green the waves intensifying into shorter ripples.

The black hole opened, expanding as the vast spirals of matter, luminous bodies, asteroids and gas forming a Catherine Wheel of windmilling energy: The great galactic plug hole. The rest of pitch black space looked on, indifferent to another two life forms about to be sucked down the drain pipe.

But what could I do? We were inevitably doomed, Lyrae and I, withdrawn from the objective, mission aborted. Our lives removed forever from the vale. All of us too, my parents, my son, the Kittens and Reptoids, even the Procurator. Our fate destined by the ineluctable modality we'd either be vapourised by a dying sun or warped to a jelly by the all consuming tidal forces of darkness. We were nearing the event horizon and I felt nothing, No up down or back to front, no north or south, right or wrong.

Then it happened.

A pull, a tug on the line, a strand of pressure in my consciousness, just a slight whisper, and all those distant stars I would never fly to, all this volatile gas that would never feel the pleasure of a good burp or fart started to clear. The universe turned lonely black and I beheld the awesome, primordial power of the unknown.

I was slowly revolving, tumbling round and around in freefall. The matter circulating around the hole didn't seem to enter this mysterious portal. No, in fact the light being sucked in was repelled, pivoted and cast back in a constant game of throw and catch.

I had no body, I had no feeling I had nothing except these words which spun like the nodes of a spider's web. When I attempted to grab some crumb of comprehension a voice from the density rumbled:

'Welcome piss boy.'

That was when I really panicked.

'Don't worry, there's no need to be frightened, we both know the vanity of that weakness. In the end you all return to me, all you who oppose or follow, you are all conned. Before I crush you from existence, there are a few irregularities we need to address.'

He sounded like the Procurator Fiscal in a Monday morning review session which oddly assuaged my terror.

'Firstly, for the loss of two hundred Sken embryos, you will endure a galactic cycle of the greatest hits of Norye.

Second, the damage to a fleet of Reptoid gunships, I will tear every memory node by node until you are a howling vacuum of despair.

Third-'

I spied my hands; they had changed to another colour, another frequency.

A delightfully calm and refreshing blue.

I raised my sight to this speculative black mass.

'Er, hold on, hold it, excuse me, but who may I ask exactly are you? If I'm going to be tortured for doing my job, I can just go back and report to syndicate headquarters. Otherwise shut your hole you great gaseous ass and either release me or let me revolve in this carousel for all eternity in peace!'

Brave words for someone spinning helplessly before the demiurge, I thought. I'd had enough: Sken embryos, snotty Procurators, Kitts and Reptoids, broken paradises, bent officials, following a cursed plasmoball team and a kid who was a rotten brat.

'I am Karel. The presence you in all your imbecilic folly met when you were a mere undergraduate at your Academy. I've been watching you, all your miserable days. Every lost love, all those botched missions, the Procurator's belittling review stages, your malodorous intestines, the-'

'All right, I get the picture.'

I detected that at any nanosecond I could be obliterated, swallowed and wiped clean. Every record and fingerprint and stain on clean porcelain sterilized forever. Here I was; an insignificant piece of flea excrement on the back of a wooly Ogdalon. What did I have to lose?

'Oh, right, fine, thanks, you see I thought I was dealing with some katabatic demiurge, a cosmic overlord or the prince of darkness. Not an inadequate, petty minded penny pinching voyeur.'

A deafening roar, a big bang of thunder and fiery sputum burst from the chasm. Entire star clusters tailspun into the revolving darkness. The voice boomed again.

'What little good do-gooding does you?'

Yet, there I was, holding my own in the pit of doom.

'I've been tailing you. Donovan, the service station canteen, Cooper, Deadwood...Oh and it was I who engineered the plasmaball final, I who sucked the ball into your rival's goal.'

The bastard!

This was war.

'Come on then? What's behind you, eh, who pulls your strings?'

'How dare you! You lower grade biomass, you like every oxygen breathing dullard struggle to exist in this eternal combustion. Even on your pitiful planet you mewl for constant attention, needs and procedures. You are born helpless and die filled with regret for what did and didn't do. Now, come to me...'

I listened, drinking in his speech without swallowing. The engulfing pressure was incomprehensible. He was right. I was weak: My mum and dad I sneered at, my son and his mother, who I abandoned to the fate of the stars. Their lives tainted by my blind groping fingers. All those flights logged, the vain arrests and convictions melted into his back heart. On a loose whim I heard myself; the last dregs sing an incomprehensible song. I couldn't remember the verse or chorus, only the absurd scat.

So it continued for how long...stuck in this merry-go-round with all the other gasses, locked in a kaleidoscopic wheel of incandescent matter and egregious squabbling: The consuming emptiness gorging upon itself and everything around it. I had nothing to do.

So I hung around.

Then, that comforting sense, the enlightening dawn, the motivating fire, our infinite power condensed into a priceless resource.

I was bored.

There was a violent shift in the gravitational pull. I heard/felt/knew something was snapping at my what? My aliveness? A growing malevolence, something not simply indifferent to living things but a, an evil intent, hell bent on clinical destruction. There was no other means to describe this phenomenon.

He remembered me all right. The sniveling snitch, the clumsy oaf who spilt his embryos, the obdurate fool who presumed he could bandy insults with him. He tightened his pull and I immediately sensed a strand of my own memory snapping. I saw my parent's faces spill into the abyss but couldn't remember their names, the Colorado boys who urinated on me in the mine, my son and his mother, the Insectoid who was head of the Syndicate. Karel was omnipresent, snapping each memory, even those I forgot or discarded. All my hates, the hatred of hates, all those irritations, incrementally dispersed; the loathing that blots all stars.

Chapter 26

I was a mere babe, helpless in his grip, naked with all the eyes of all the worlds, mocking and jeering. I resisted, pulled myself back, retreated into my own warm darkness, the comfort of cynicism and doubt.

These too were being sucked like dust in a turbine. I tried to scream but had no voice, tried to curse but found no words: Every picture popping like bubbles, each particle dropped in the mine.

He'd reached the central strands, four nodes holding me together. The air inside me blew, the water dried, the fire cooled, the earth melted.

Karel took everything.

I had nothing...I was nothing. With no sense of whom I was, no warm purpose to my life except facing the screaming void I then knew without walls or roof or floor I was unutterably mad.

Yet, there still remained that gentle pressure. The drag of the hole hadn't quite claimed me. It was a brief flicker, a passing flash of honey and cream.

My hands turned purple.

I was pulled back from the whirlpool again.

Lyrae.

I saw the ship near the event horizon, within seconds she would end up as a bowl of cat food. I saw again all light sucked in, rebound, whirl and whirl, be rinsed around the black circumference and repeat...ad infinitum.

The pressure ceased.

Karel fell as silent as the stars around him. My thoughts dried up. I felt nothing; I was as empty as the space between my atoms. In this easy stillness I was at peace. As soon as my mind died, my density fluctuations occurred as the big three, the neutrons, protons and electrons did their merry dance as hydrogen, helium and lithium in me spontaneously exploded into the void.

He asked me a simple question and I gave him a simple answer.

'You aren't real you big bag of wind.'

The trillions of particles gravitating in cyclonic gyration, wheeled towards the hole, turned and scattered out into the cosmos. Again the hole sucked, the light turned, forming the spiral arms in thoughtless distance before expanding outwards. And so on, and so forth...

'I've got my eye on you boy. You watch your back.' The abyss roared.

'Asshole!' I retorted.

I pulled myself together. Everyone I loved, I cared for returning to my magnetic pull. My wavelengths and electrons, protons atoms: All returning in a gently inverted explosion. When the million or so tiny golden globes integrated back into I assumed my stomach, I performed an about face and marched off.

Everything that passed between us reversed. My magical web of memories reassembled, strand by strand by node. I felt stronger, solid; the spiraling light being drawn into the black hole was deflecting, shooting off again and spinning back into space. I was flying backwards, a magnetic resistance, further from the hole, closer to the ship, drifting softly, gently like falling ash. I swam upstream, flowing between the rocks and extraordinary flares. The Zelan ship was suspended, hovering on the threshold of the whirlpool, a twisting double helix, before the dust devil himself.

Drifting towards her now, was it excitement charging through my thoughts? I glanced where I thought my hands were and there, six fingers of translucent cyan, splayed between the ship and my face. My face, my puckered lips, forehead straining with concentrated effort. I was breathing, quick breaths of anticipation, my legs kicked hard, surging myself forward as the blooming buds flowered in my belly.

With each flicker of desire I was propelled further from oblivion, pushing the ship clear of the event horizon.

I eventually passed through the roof, in seconds or centuries (gravitational time dilation?). It didn't matter I was returning to Lyrae still shaking my inert body through the roof before full atomic cohesion took hold.

I opened my eyes to the perennial smile of my friend, purring as she stroked my hair. In that entire super space-time I was gone, she'd fashioned a sling from Agate's sleeve and scrupulously washed her face.

'How you doing sport?'

I made an effort to sit up.

My body mind and spirit was filled with the delicious warmth that opens buds, turns the tides and lights the stars. Or so my dad says.

'Fine, just a little tired.'

'Relax. We're out of danger; the ship's reversing her course.'

My eyes refocused on her fuzzy face. I blew her a kiss and winked.

'I got the black eyed blues.' I drawled,

That indelible grin broke into cackling laughter.

'You were well out of it, howling and barking some absolute nonsense. I thought I'd lost you.'

Her light hands were all I needed. We only shared a passing glance in that moment but she saw me. She knew, I knew...

She insisted I remain lying while she oversaw the course. We were heading back to the gigantic asteroid, maintaining three quarters velocity with all systems optimal, ripping through the forbidden territory wingless but on a prayer the Zelans didn't rumble us. Whenever a hostile presence appeared on radar the ship wheeled and pitched, dancing smart until we cleared the threat.

We landed beside the corvette, hidden behind a serrated ridge. Before we transferred the two humans on board, Lyrae and I enacted one of the more idiosyncratic human customs. We embraced long and firm, resting our foreheads on the other's shoulders. We detached delicately matching our reciprocal gaze with silence. I looked to the dome, the entry panel open, the lights were bleeping desperately. I knew what we had to do.

The corvette was running on a fraction of power. She took off, climbed above the Zelan vessel and swung round. She checked the cannon reserves: Enough for one final deadly blast. She positioned our ship into an attack dive and hit full throttle. The corvette roared into a ferocious swoop and she rested her finger on the fire button.

Lyrae pushed the control stick hard left and we screamed for home, leaving the ship containing the four brains on the asteroid to the blind fate of the distant stars.

Chapter 27

It took half a day of mumbled explanations and borrowed favours for the Syndicate maintenance crew to authorize a full respray and even greater cajoling and implied bribes for the quartermaster to issue us new uniforms. The badges would have to wait that wee bit longer.

We spent two days recuperating in the medical department of Sinatra 5. The soft mattress was bliss as I waited for the penultimate scan and prep for the subcutaneous operation on my laser burned cheek. It would be another forty eight hours for a complete reconstruction the med officer advised. He concluded my mind might take a while though but with consistent therapy sessions I ought to be fully functional within a month or two.

Lyrae dropped by my bedside on the final evening. She brought me a bowl of fried vaco chips and a sparkling bottle of avajuice.

'You ought to get a commendation for this you know,' she mouthed through a handful of chips.

'And you deserve a first class, with honours, top of the tree merit.' I sipped the avajuice in short bursts. It was the first time I tried it. Nice. I'd always spurned it because of the patronising adverts. Mind you, it was a child's beverage after all. I placed the bottle on the side table and waited until she finished her packet of chips.

'You are...going back?'

She rolled the packet between her palms. A disposodroid appeared, took the empty packet then left as quickly as it arrived.

She brushed some of the chip dust from her palms then licked her fingers. She gulped her Lactrodrene down to the dregs.

'We'll see. I might let it pass.'

We spent the next day, just hours after the final treatment on my face touring the glades. They led to a narrow path leading to the mountain. Climbing the dusty path was thirsty work so we stopped beside a stream pouring into a small waterfall on some flat rocks. I held my fingers under the water until they were numb. Lyrae scooped a palmful and slurped noisily.

'I hope they stick us together again. What's the chances?'

I ogled her shoulder, thinking the very same.

'Well, sometimes they do, if the partnerships a success.'

'Which it is.'

'Yes. '

She took another slurp of the sparkling stream while I dried my hands.

'Lyrae.'

'Mm.'

'I. we, that is our...'

She bowed her head to catch my vague eyes.

'Go on.'

My chest was churning wickedly. I needed another heart to balance the torrent of blood. My feet were tingling. I freed my gaze, focusing on the maem flower beside the stream, obviously imported from Elyssia. Her pink and violet leaves were surfing the breeze, cooing an afternoon song. I never saw before how beautiful she was. My heart ached for home.

'Never mind.'

I stood up to try and get the flow going. Distribute the fluid.

'Let's go.'

It was night when we boarded the gleaming, replenished corvette. Leaving the planet's orbit I scrutinized the hundred pinpricks of shimmering stars from the Stellaport window. It would take at least a week before we returned to face the wrath of the Procurator. The parity gained in snaffling the two runaways outweighed the numerous violations and indiscretions cut against my name.

In the seconds while we waited for orbital clearance, the docking release procedure commenced. Lyrae asked me 'By the way, what was that you were jabbering on about while you were spark out.' I shrugged.

'I don't know. Something in old Elyssian. Do bee do bee do.'

Lyrae bowed her head, smirking. I joined in, releasing a loud guffaw.

'Corny eh?' I hooted through the mirth.

When the dock gates opened fully and all lights turned green we breezed from the massive platforms high above the tangle of neon threads bundled within the sprawl of Sinatra. We had a fair journey ahead of us: I Couldn't wait to return home.

'Here we go,' I said as we raced to the million sparkles and a hell of a space before us.

Chapter 28

 The lecture theatre was filled wall to wall with rows of council staff and families of graduates. The first three rows consisted of the Association executives and directors including the Lord Advocate and Procurator Fiscal. Flanking them were Office Marshalls and moderators: Seated to their rear; the rank and file of marshalls, sheriffs and rangers. Behind them the families and friends of that handful who sweated, pulled muscles, read Multiverse law until their eyes bled and risked their lives for this moment; the newly badged, stood saluting the congregation. Lyrae was the shortest among the assorted humans and Fandorians and Xltens but she stood immobile, never switching her pupils from the back wall.

Each high official reinforced the purpose of the Associated Species Syndicate for the prosperity and stability of the concomitant systems. The last official emphasized the important roles sheriff's played in the body, scrolling his tendril across the assembly before shuffling back to his seat.

Finally the Presidente del Consiglio rose and was aided to the stage by two hefty looking goons. He awarded the Procurator a golden badge, proclaiming the successful return of two of the galaxy's most dangerous criminals and the subsequent drop in statistics. He insisted the Procurator give a brief speech which he did without pause.

'Your Elementary goodness, Syndicate members, new graduates I thank you. I accept not this badge for myself, but for the brave and unselfish souls out there, risking death to make this enterprising universe a safer prospect. I stand with you fellow Peacekeepers in the opposition of those who seek to destroy our needs, our freedom of choice, our right, our destiny to profit from the bounty set before us, to iron out the weak and chastise the lazy, the feckless and the renegade few who spoil our well earned progress and our right to a bit of starshine.'

I yawned long and loud, returning three feeble handclaps while he waffled on.

When the speeches and applause and praise dispensed she ran towards me. I was leaning against the theridium doorframe. We hugged and I kissed her, inhaling the comforting musk from her cheek.

'It's no mean feat to pass that course, well done.'

She scanned my civvies.

'You off duty? I'd have thought you would be in your blues for this?'

She was referring to my airy white shirt and baggy burgundy trousers, tucked into knee high boots.

'I came to see you. Only you. I, I've um...'

'You've what?'

I scratched my bare chest, casting a glance into the hall. The Procurator was ambling beside the stage nodding to a grinning Macbeth.

'I've decided to pursue another direction.'

I returned to her golden eyes then watched her shoulder so I could see her clearly.

'I've got to go.'

Her pupils were locked on, my belly quivered. There was no visible response, no twitch of whisker or furrow of brow. She was fatefully serious.

'It's your son, isn't it?'

Macbeth's laughter echoed across the room.

'And other things.'

We walked the memorial gardens that afternoon, as I outlined my meagre reasons for quitting. As the sun sunk, long shadows from the trees and headstones titled upon us. I congratulated her for the tenth time and wished her a planetful of luck and success. Cold night arrived swiftly and I escorted her to the barracks.

The forecourt was swilling with graduates, a few old timers and a core of supervisors basking in their protégées success. Some hangers on, civs who through commercial and contractual links, cluttered up the entrance, assuming their fragile bonds with us would tie them to a sheltered life or protect them from the unseen horrors. They laughed loudest and huddled around the storytelling circles.

As I inhaled my breath stuttered and I shivered in the chill. I spotted Dane Sligot and Stevie Wandsworth, two fellow students in my Masters year. We all woke up the day after graduation on a freighter bound for Canis Major...

I've made another foolhardy decision haven't I?

I smiled before Lyrae. Let's not make another one. I tapped my foot to hide the growing shakes in my leg. Come on, don't be a piss boy. Say it. My knees trembled uncontrollably.

'All the best, Lyrae. Do keep in touch.'

Her face was puzzled.

'You're not coming in for a drink?'

Pounding music was already erupting from the open windows. The chink of bottle on glass, anecdotes and meeting old colleagues was an appealing prospect. I felt her radiance touch my open neck, forming a warm bubble against the cool air. My belly ached, my breathing withered, my feet were splitting in half.

'I'm catching the late transporter to Elyssia.'

The corners of her eyes folded, her left ear twitched.

'But we're a good team; we make a great partnership, yeah?'

Where's a black hole when you need one.

We stood on even ground, squared within trim grass split by crazy paving. I shrugged while her face relaxed from expectancy to mild resignation.

Neither of us could speak the word so smothered in our hearts. I kissed her once more and turned, walking through the sentry droids for the last time. My feet were being stung by a million little barbs. When I stepped through the gates onto the busy central thoroughfare, I stopped, the tip of a rock peeping above a torrent. My chest was ablaze with a terrifying feeling I didn't understand. Go on you idiot, tell her I heard an urgent voice growl.

I turned but she was gone, lost forever in the music and laughter.

Chapter 29

The deluge of pedestrians urged me far from the gates. I kept glancing back to see if she was there but the tide was overwhelming. I reached for a holovid platform displaying a trailer for a new drama serial, interspersed with revolving messages to live life, be happy and buy a Sondisc. A gang of adolescent Mangoeurs shoved past, one of their elbows catching me in the midriff. Winded, I stumbled to the underground Stellaport shuttle. There was one every hour. I still had time.

My feet kept flapping forward, heaving my chest and throbbing forehead. In a daze I stubbed my fingers on my Sondisc to pay and boarded a half empty carriage. My belly was leaden with damp trembling as I watched the doors close.

The shuttle rocketed to the Stellaport, much faster than usual. I tried to stifle the bitterness rising in my throat, covered my eyes from the prying passengers. I needed a space, a small still empty space to be. Twisting through the aisle I jogged to the toilet just as the first tears broke.

Out of order.

Hitting my head on the cold metal plate, I pressed my juddering chest to the scratched surface oblivious to the honking and hooting of amusement from my accompanying passengers. When I rubbed my eyes clear the compartment was still blurry. I rubbed my face and pushed hard into my sockets blinked and widened the skin around my eyes. Still there was a faint fuzzy radiance. Then I slowly discerned...the floor was solid, there were scuff marks and footprints, the outline of the seats remained edged and firm.

The haze was emanating from my fellow passengers.

The pair nearest me who tittered through my sobbing fit was conversing in low barks. A murky yellowish fog clung around their bellies. An insectoid mother holding her baby sat beneath a pearlescent cloud. An old human fumbling in his satchel was awash in grey wisps. Clusters of sliver particles swarmed around some hands while undulating wavelengths of differing frequencies rippled from the brows of most. I closed my eyes and upon opening them I saw the same effects, albeit with slight variations in tone and rhythm.

The old human slipped off his seat a collapsing pile of dirty laundry. As I stooped to help him the grey wisps lightened in the way sunshine finally breaks through cloud. I searched for assistance around the carriage but saw only the wavelengths from those close turn jagged, like cracked glass. Bizarrely I heard a multitude of voices in my head translate the rough vibrations: *'Not my problem,'* *'I wouldn't embarrass myself like that,'* *'Should be able to look after themselves,'* *'totally counterproductive,'* *'well, someone else is dealing with it.'*

When I hoisted the old man back to his seat he lifted his chin and smiled, a nodding thanks. The sun dazzled my vision and I patted him on the shoulder, resuming my place beside the toilet.

As the shuttle arrived at the Stellaport the currents exploded into a tidal wave of dark blue panic. I waited with the old man, eventually helping him off when the carriage was empty.

In the Stellaport lounge I passed the time reading the ocean of biomagnetic currents. Harassed families with their collective rainbow fields, the solo business passengers all metallic braces and hard wires and the odd smuggler, whose bellies churned with murky ochre. Soon my eyes grew gritty. Closing them I settled back into the film of skin wrapping my flesh and bones. When they were reopened the visions of multiple wavelengths had gone.

Two sheriffs were seated at a distant table, sipping their drink. They appeared oblivious, indifferent even, to the cacophony and stampede around them. Although they seemed like two display dummies, inured to the micro troubles of the other passengers, they'd be zoned in to every ripple and rumble. Awake to the slightest suspicious move. They were both Antarians from the Scorpius constellation. Good in a fight, handy pilots. They fastidiously tidied their table, even brushing down the seats and checking the floor for crumbs. My soul reeled. I'd made another wrong decision. I should be with them, flying a cruiser into a pirate's lair. The sting of regret cooled when saw me and joined me in the empty seats to my left.

'Luten, isn't it?' The female asked.

'Yes, that's right. Do I know you?'

They both laughed in their harsh, scraping manner.

'No, we know you. The renegade job. We heard the proc today, lapping up the honours. We know the deal.'

I was genuinely alarmed. 'How?'

The female tapped her temple. 'We know, Lute' her voice hissed inside my head.

'What you up to now? Bounty hunting? PD work? Convoy escort? Dude with your hands would be in great demand.'

I relaxed slightly. I felt a genuine warmth radiate from their hard carapaces.

Well. I don't know, got a couple of things, unfinished business.'

'Yeah, we hear you. Gotta go. Look, you need any back up, let us know. Name's Lennana, this is Tirq.'

'Hi.'

'Hello.'

'Hope you find what you're hunting.'

'Yes, yes, thank you.'

'Watch your ass out there.'

I will, I most certainly will.

They left with a wave and smiles when my departure was announced. Two boarding queues were filing through the gates. I stood in the shortest queue which took longest to board. I didn't mind, I made the right choice.

I found an empty compartment on the transporter to myself. Before me all the stars and planets and black holes waited. The strange swelling in my chest which had been building since I walked through the Academy gates receded. I had crossed the forbidden territory, I'm sure my father would have a heap of platitudes to cover that, but I needed his and my mother's help, my people's help for where I needed to go now. The ethylene cry in my guts was a pleasurable tear. The old squirming started up, my bowels weakened, but instead of the hot oil jetting from my intestines, my belly relaxed into a quiet purr. My digestion was turning over. The stewardess offered me a plate of delicious fry or a freshly chopped green mess. I chose the salad. We were cleared for takeoff and as we fooled old gravity, roaring out of orbit I serenely observed my shiny palms.

Just before the ship entered Paraspace, I spoke to the constellations drifting past the oblong window. 'Somewhere, wherever you are, I'll find you again' I snorted, placed my loose fingers on my placid belly then settled into a fecund and dream filled sleep.

Made in the USA
Middletown, DE
10 June 2017